THE SPACE BETWEEN US

based on a film by Jennifer DiMarco

a novelization by
Michelle Lee

BLUE FORGE PRESS
Port Orchard · Washington

*because stories should exist
for everyone*

The Space Between Us

based on a film by Jennifer DiMarco

a novelization by
Michelle Lee

Chapter One

Day 1

Raindrops fell on the balconies that hovered over the sidewalk of a large apartment building. Gray and dismal skies matched the monochromatic scene of the concrete structures in the area. The weather was typical for a winter day in the Pacific Northwest.

On the second floor, Alison, wearing a goose-down puffy olive-green jacket, carried a cloth bag of groceries away from her front door to her car. Her expression was calm, but if you looked closely at her eyes, you could see there were thousands of thoughts going through her head.

Life wasn't all colorful clothes, sunny personalities, and roses coming up all the time—even if that's what Alison tried to portray each day. Life had worn her down, yet she did everything in her power to try and maintain a positive outlook and remain a good role model for her children. She wanted them to know that kindness mattered, and a gentle touch could go a long way.

She did her best to be a good parent to her twins, and some days, she felt like she missed the mark. This yearly getaway was her opportunity to try and redeem some of those moments where she felt like she'd let her children down.

It was true that Alison was a mostly optimistic person, she wore her heart on her sleeve, and she genuinely cared about people. Lately, it all seemed to be more hassle than it was worth when dealing with love, the exception to that being her kids. Yet, she held on, struggled, and stubbornly carried that hope with her everywhere she went.

Following behind Alison were her twins that carried their suitcases with luggage tags that bore their names, Taylor and Griffin. They each wore bright anticipatory smiles on their faces. Something that made Alison proud when she looked at them. As far as kids went, she thought she had the best.

Taylor was naturally down to earth with an adventurous spirit and passion in her soul. On this trip, she had a Super 8 camera she brought that she had strapped over her shoulder and filmed their journey as they went along. Taylor had big dreams of being a producer and creating films. She was good at it, too. Alison loved that creative streak and a sharp eye for things that spoke to Taylor and said, 'create me.'

Griffin sported a raspberry-colored beret on his head, a black jacket, and carried a copy of Beat Poet Magazine and his hardback poetry portfolio with a pen in his hand. He had a hipster vibe, yet Griffin was authentic and genuine, wore his heart on his sleeve, and had a flamboyant and unapologetic personality. His dreams were of being a writer. And what a way with words he had. Alison felt positive that she would be reading a book he wrote someday.

Though she hadn't carried the twins herself, they were hers in every other sense of the word. She'd raised them, loved them, fed them, was there for them, and encouraged them. Alison stopped herself from mentally heading down that track. This trip was supposed to be about Griffin and his opportunity, and all she could do was hope that the people he needed to be there for him were there.

Today, Griffin was excited but also felt a touch nervous. He paused at the railing before heading down the stairs, lost in thought. It was his last year to compete in the poetry festival, and Griffin so badly wanted to win. His heart and soul were in his words, and he knew they would resonate with someone if he could get over his stage fright and nerves about speaking in front of people. Easier said than done, and he wasn't sure he was on the same level as the reigning champion.

Having descended a few stairs outside, Alison managed to pull car keys out of her pocket without dropping anything. She passed in front of Taylor's camera on her way down, not giving it a second thought as she'd grown used to it. After a few more steps, she noticed that Griffin wasn't with them and stopped to look back, making sure he was okay. That caused Taylor to turn expectantly towards her brother, her camera moving with her. Griffin exhaled a nervous breath and gave himself an internal pep talk. It was his year; he could feel it. Between thoughts that rumbled through his head, Griffin noticed Taylor waiting for him. With a bit of smile, a nod reassuring himself that he could achieve his goal, he continued down the stairs toward her.

At the bottom of the stairs, they lugged their bags toward the car. Taylor and Griffin helped Alison load their luggage and groceries into the back of their red Toyota SUV. From all appearances, the three were a happy and close family, with love in their hearts. A happy family headed out on a trip as so many other families do this time of year. The assumption wouldn't be wrong.

They each got in the car, with the twins sitting in the back seat. Taylor kept her Super 8 camera next to her and filmed while Griffin had his magazine and portfolio sitting on his lap. His eyes were rereading the words printed as if he hadn't already memorized every word of the poem he would perform for the preliminaries of the competition.

All of them in their own worlds, alone, but together. Though Alison's heart was heavy, she went out of her way to ensure that her kids wouldn't notice what she worked so hard on keeping locked up tight.

At a different house not terribly far away, up a steep driveway, Roslyn carried two suitcases to her silver Toyota SUV parked in front of her garage. Her steps were quick to avoid getting soaked by the rain, though she didn't try too hard; it was only water. She wasn't a prissy woman worried about her hair getting messed up.

The back of the vehicle was already opened, and inside lay a bag full of toiletries. Roslyn kept them separate now after a bottle of shampoo broke open inside a suitcase once—oh, the mess that caused. She got the two bags settled in the back and ran her hands down her somewhat masculine clothes. She felt a little dowdy and worried what Miles would think, even if she shouldn't care.

Her goose-down puffy olive green kept her warm, though, and she loved it. Her pants were utilitarian and suited most circumstances she might find herself in, and the plain white shirt was equally universal. Roslyn didn't even know why the thoughts about how she looked mattered. She'd never been a fashionista-type person.

Orion, Roslyn's young son, darted past her to the vehicle carrying his tinker case. It was a medium-sized hard case with a handle. It's where he held the items he currently tinkered with and created new inventions from the gadgets and gizmos he kept in there. He pushed his round glasses back up his face, ran to the passenger side of the SUV with youthful energy, let himself in, and settled into his seat.

After ensuring everything was tucked inside, Roslyn closed the back, made her way to the driver's side door, and got in. Her movements were automatic, like she had pushed an autopilot button. Roslyn's body knew what she needed to do, but her brain was somewhere else focused on hundreds of other things. One thing remained constant, Roslyn smiled and thought again about how lucky she was to have a son like Orion.

Roslyn was strong, reliable, stable, yet, there was evidence of an internal struggle. Her face bore signs of tension and unease, the pursed lips, creases between her eyes, and the tight, pinched look she wore. Still, she buckled up, ensured Orion was secure and backed down and out of the long, steep driveway.

Roslyn was doing her best to keep the nervous energy from Orion, but kids had a way of seeing things parents didn't want them to. Orion knew why his mother was worried. She hadn't seen his father since they got divorced. He'd been worried about his mom but wasn't sure how to bring it up with her. She didn't talk about her own issues much; she took care of others. He pushed his glasses up his nose again and watched her when she wasn't looking; he took careful mental notes.

On interstate ninety, rural Washington sped by at seventy miles an hour. Driving over the mountain passes was always scenic, with the abundance of green trees, steep rocky cliffs, and deep ravines. Even on dreary days, the rugged natural beauty was stunning.

Despite nature doing its best to impress the travelers, Alison largely ignored the picturesque landscape, concentrated on the road, and did her best to learn while she traversed the pass.

Hello, students, and welcome to Culinary Arts 101, Professor Weston said.

Alison drove as she intently listened to the podcast class she was taking.

This is class nine of your remote learning experience with Peninsula University, Professor Weston went on.

In the backseat, Griffin sat reading his Beat Poet Magazine for the umpteenth time. It was as if he didn't hear the podcast at all. He immersed himself in the stories and verses in the magazine that Dax Linn graced the cover of, even though he'd already read it cover to cover several times.

Next to her brother, Taylor silently filmed Griffin

reading the literature as Professor Weston droned on.

As always: Congratulations. You've decided to explore a new career...

Feeling watched, Griffin glanced over at his sister, and, seeing the camera, he gave her a crooked grin. Caught in the act, Taylor lowered the camera and smiled back at her brother. They remained silent so as not to disturb their mother.

...and take control of your future. Professor Weston paused for dramatic effect. *Let's begin.*

Through the concrete jungle of downtown Seattle on interstate five, Roslyn drove through the traffic and hardly noticed the towering skyscrapers that made up the Seattle skyline. From the speakers of her car, the automated phone assistant informed her of her messages.

You have, a pause, *four,* pause, *messages from,* a final pause, *William Patterson.*

Roslyn continued to drive and paid no attention to the surroundings other than the traffic around her as she listened to the first message.

No, no, no, no, no! You can't leave town right now, Roslyn! William Patterson cried out insistently from the recorded message; his voice was panicked.

In the backseat, Orion had his tinker case opened on his lap. His cell phone was connected to an external battery via his charging cable to a small robot that he worked on completing. He was close to being finished with the little project.

My deadline is only a week away! I need my editor, Roslyn! I need you—

The sound of a machine beeping filled the car. The

robotic voice of the phone assistant came back on.

Message deleted. You have no further messages.

Having heard that, Orion set free a small smile and continued his tinkering as his mom drove. It kept him busy, and it was one of his favorite things to do. Plus, he excelled at it.

A few miles later, Roslyn pulled into a McDonald's and stared at the drive-thru menu as her order got repeated back to her.

That's a Filet-a-fish, a large fry, a ten-piece chicken nuggets, and two small Cokes. That'll be ten seventy-seven at the first window.

Roslyn pulled the car forward and inched closer to the window. She waited somewhat patiently for their turn to pay and then received the food. It wasn't the healthiest of meals for them, but it was food that would sustain them. She needed the protein, and if she was honest, the French fries were comfort food.

After they received their meal, Roslyn parked the car in the parking lot and passed Orion's food back to him. She picked at her fries while Orion munched happily on his nuggets with an occasional glance out the window. The rain was on and off, and the clouds moved swiftly in the sky.

When his phone dinged with a text message, he glanced down at his phone to see a text from his father, Miles Thomas. He had responded to Orion's earlier text.

We're on our way, Daddy :), Orion had sent.

Can't wait to see your newest invention, kiddo. Tell Mommy to drive safely; Miles had texted back.

Orion looked up from his phone to look at his mother eating fries. He considered passing the message along but ultimately decided not to. He didn't want her to tense up any more than she already was. Orion returned to eating his nuggets instead and worried about his mother again. He intuitively knew that repeating his father's message would upset her.

Roslyn, unaware of the message, took a drink of her soda. She had one of those thousand-yard stares; she was so deep into her thoughts. Her eating was robotic and automatic, a practiced move from years of eating on the go while she did other things. Multi-tasking was her way of life between work and Orion's schedule.

Once she finished, she started the car, and slowly backed out of her parking spot, and got back on the road to their destination. The silence didn't bother either of them.

Alison checked her mirrors and slowly took the exit that approached for a rest area. The sign showed that picnic tables were available, and she'd packed a lunch for them that was perfect for a small picnic. It would be great for all of them to get out and stretch and move around a bit. The rain had let off, and while it was overcast, it wasn't unpleasant.

She pulled into a parking spot, got out, stretched out the kinks, and then walked around the back to unpack the food she'd brought along. She grabbed a bag containing three different colored bento boxes. She unwrapped each one and removed the lids, displaying beautifully crafted rice paper wrapped vegetarian spring rolls, a small roll, and a chocolate truffle. Each hand made with the skills she'd been honing with her podcast. Alison was rather proud of what she had accomplished.

The kids sat down across the table from her and happily dove into the food. Taylor's Super 8 camera rested on the table beside her, never far out of her reach, and Griffin's magazine and portfolio lie off to the side of his food, also quickly accessible. For both kids, they liked to say you never knew when inspiration would strike. They loved the packed lunch and savored each bite their mother had taken the time to make.

Alison ate distractedly; as she picked up her phone and sent a text to Jac Wylie. *Will you be there?* Alison texted. Her frustration mounted, and it was getting harder to swallow.

She saw the message had gotten read, but no response. She waited a few more moments before she followed it up with another text. *Jac?* When there was still nothing, she set the phone down, annoyed. Alison did everything she could to keep the emotions from showing on her face and went back to eating. The food had lost its taste at that point. It could have been cardboard for all Alison knew.

Griffin watched his mother with concern. He shot a disappointed look at the discarded phone and then back to Alison. Even if he were blind, he would have noticed the hurt and anxiety that riddled his mom.

Taylor, attuned to her brother, noticed Griffin's concern and wondered what was up. She'd obviously missed something because Griffin seemed agitated to some degree; however, not overly so. The three of them sat there in silence and finished their meal before heading back out on the road. Taylor vowed to herself to keep a closer eye on her mom and brother.

Roslyn drove slowly down the unfamiliar street. She knew the road was here somewhere. Roslyn craned her neck to read the signs and looked for the turn. Finally spotting it, she flipped on her right turn signal. Since Orion was asleep in the back seat with his tinker case on his lap, Roslyn made the turn gently, went down a steep driveway, and pulled in front of a two-car garage.

She parked in front of the left garage and glanced over at the cottage on the right. It was cozy looking, she supposed. Her outlook wasn't the brightest at the moment due to having to deal with her ex-husband, but she needed to make the best of it for Orion's sake. He'd been looking forward to this little trip for a while now.

Alison arrived from the opposite direction that Roslyn had been, and she flipped on her left turn signal. The way was ingrained into her memory. They'd been traveling this way six or seven years; previous vacations—all for Griffin to compete in the festival that meant so much to him.

Griffin was asleep on the back seat with the portfolio open on his lap and the magazine tucked under it. His head was tipped back and leaned against the window. Taylor had her Super 8 on and focused on the open portfolio to capture Griffin's words for her film. He'd fallen asleep with the pen still in his hand, and she wanted to get it all:

This yearly journey.
So much the same
when everything
has changed.

It is the last year.

As Alison turned the car, the Super 8 jolted, and Taylor lowered the camera to look out the front window. She smiled as they drove down the steep drive towards the familiar cottage. Taylor's eyebrows furrowed in confusion as she spotted the other car in the driveway as Alison pulled in front of the garage door on the other side of the stranger's vehicle.

Alison gave a confused look at Roslyn as she walked with purpose around her gray SUV to the opened back and pulled out luggage. Something wasn't right with this picture, and an unsettled feeling landed with a brick in the pit of her stomach.

Roslyn bore an equally puzzled expression. An SUV identical to hers except in color pulled partly next to the right of her vehicle. She immediately began walking toward the driver's side window as Alison killed the engine and lowered her window. Roslyn stared at the soft, feminine woman behind the wheel with purple hair, and something stirred in her gut.

"Hi. You're in 7419?" Alison asked, bewildered.

"I hope so," Roslyn answered with a frown somewhere between amused and confused. "That's what I rented."

Alison remained in the car but grew upset and did her best to mask it. "Really? So did I." She wondered what the other woman found so amusing with the situation.

Roslyn's face crinkled in confusion, though she remained polite. *What the heck?!* she thought to herself.

Chapter Two

Roslyn walked away from Alison's SUV and back to her own, pulling her phone out of her pocket. Her stride was long, and her steps fell heavy as her mind couldn't make up whether she was angry, irritated, or amused by the apparent mix-up.

Alison got out of her vehicle, took her phone out, and looked for a spot that had reception. Her previous years at this location had taught her that her carrier had spotty service here. What she wouldn't give to be on the cottage's deck she'd been staying at for the past six or seven years, staring down at the beautiful wooded view of the river.

Roslyn was already on the phone with the eBnB agent she'd used to book the cottage, and her tone of voice was less than pleasant. "You've got to be kidding me!" she barked out with an exasperated and unamused tone while she paced.

Taylor and Griffin had gotten out of the SUV, stood helplessly, and looked shell-shocked. Taylor had her camera slung over her shoulder, wondering if she should film, and Griffin clutched his portfolio and magazine to his chest, casting looks between the two vehicles. They glanced over at their mom, who was now on the phone and using a calm if slightly irritated voice.

"Yes, I'm still here," Alison replied calmly. Inside she was panicking and trying to hold it together. "Thank you." She stood with the river and trees to her back, afraid to get her hopes up that they'd be staying here. Not looking at them might help soften the blow; at least, that's what she kept telling herself. "I'm sorry. I'm just not sure how this could have happened. We've rented the same cottage for the past six years." Alison paused a moment, listening to the bluster that the agent spouted. "Sure. I can hold."

Roslyn stalked over to Alison assertively; her cell phone pressed to her ear and her tone aggressive. "Don't apologize to these people. You didn't—" Roslyn fell silent, mid-tirade. "Yes. I'm still right here. Standing outside the cottage, I paid twelve hundred dollars for." She listened for a moment. "What?" she snapped. Another beat of silence pounded in her ear. "Fine."

Roslyn glanced curiously over at Alison, with her purple curly hair, colorful and feminine blouse, calm voice, and her appealing curvy body. She sighed deeply and pushed down the admiration blooming in her chest. The day simply could not get more frustrating; she didn't have time for the attraction. Roslyn angrily punched the speakerphone button on her phone and held it out between the two of them.

"Go for it," Roslyn demanded in a barking tone.

"On behalf of eBnB, I apologize for this inconvenience," the agent, Trina, apologized.

"It's okay," Alison responded automatically in a placating voice. Always the peacekeeper.

"It's not," Roslyn challenged, her tone wry. In Roslyn's opinion, the apology was insincere and part of a scripted scenario that some person who wrote procedures somewhere thought of and put the proper response down on paper to get repeated to an angry customer should the situation arise.

In the kitchen of Trina's home, the flustered agent sat at her kitchen table, her laptop opened in front of her that displayed the double booking. On the other side of the table sat a dead plant and a can of pens and pencils. A framed sign hung on the wall that featured the eBnB logo of a heart and a house with the motto: Smaller. Cheaper. Better.

"I see that you both made your reservations online several months ago. Paid in full. You have the cottage Wednesday through Tuesday. Not unusual for this time of year. All of our rentals in and around Leavenworth are in very high demand with the—" Trina hurriedly told the unhappy clients and got cut off mid-sentence.

With Roslyn's phone held between them, Alison and Roslyn chimed in simultaneously with mirrored exasperated expressions plastered on their faces. "Orion Poetry Festival."

Alison randomly noticed that Roslyn's phone case

had a quote from the Robert Frost poem, The Road Not Taken. She wasn't sure why she found that interesting, but she did. Griffin liked that poem as well. But that thought had nothing to do with their situation, and she needed to focus.

"Yes. We know," Roslyn fought the urge to shout. She tried to take her cues from the unassuming woman that stood in front of her. A little calm couldn't hurt the debacle.

Trina arched an eyebrow. "But you don't know each other?"

"No," Roslyn answered irritably.

"You're sure?" Trina pressed. Something about this had raised Trina's curiosity.

Roslyn was about to lose her temper entirely on the inept agent. She was finished trying the calm approach, and the insinuation that they were lying was too much. "Look—"

Alison interrupted the angry woman before she exploded. "No. We don't know each other. Do you have anything else available? We can—"

At this point, Griffin grew agitated. "Mom!" he stepped forward in alarm. Routine was an integral part of his mental preparation for the competition. If they had to stay somewhere new, he wouldn't feel comfortable or be able to concentrate the way he needed to.

Taylor sensed her brother's panic and grabbed his arm to calm him. Griffin looked back at her and halted his momentum. He fell silent and stood anxiously next to his sister.

Alison looked stricken, but she didn't know what

else to do. Nothing about this vacation had gone the way she'd thought it would, and she hated disappointing her kids. She'd gone into this with high hopes. They hadn't even gotten inside the cottage yet, and everything had fallen apart.

Roslyn sighed in defeat and looked at Alison. "You don't have to do that." Her tone became conciliatory.

"We have to do something," Alison argued insistently. She knew how important this was to Griffin.

"Ladies?" Trina interrupted and tried to regain control of the conversation.

"This is your regular place," Roslyn said kindly, drawn in despite herself.

"Things change," Alison replied caustically. Life had taught her that lesson well.

"Excuse me!" Trina shouted through the phone, trying to get their attention.

Both Alison and Roslyn looked down at the phone in surprise at the aggressive tone. *What reason did this lady have to be angry with them?* both women thought.

Typing at her computer, Trina continued once the women fell silent. "I've got nothing until after the festival. But no one has to move. You have five guests, and the cottage sleeps six. Both families can stay, and for the trouble, I can refund half your rental fee."

Alison looked down at the phone held in Roslyn's hand, unconvinced that it was a wise idea. They knew nothing about each other. What if this woman was crazy? Hadn't she dealt with that enough already? Her usual optimism had failed her the moment she realized they'd rented the same cottage.

Roslyn, on the other hand, looked thrilled. She made good money and didn't really have to worry too much about finances because she was typically frugal. It might even grant her some time to figure out why this lady fascinated her so much. "Done!" she declared.

"I don't know," Alison hedged, uncomfortable with the thought.

"You'll hardly know we're here," Roslyn insisted, warming to the idea the more they talked.

"How did this even happen?" Alison asked helplessly, still frustrated and disappointed. She refused to look at her kids in fear of the disappointment she was positive they felt. What if this adversely affected Griffin? Taylor would be okay; she was a strong young woman.

The women heard more typing through the phone and then Trina's voice. "It appears the... system... thought you were the same party. Alison Wylie, and Roslyn Wiley."

Alison and Roslyn looked up in surprise at each other. "W-y-l-i-e," Alison spelled out automatically.

"W-i-l-e-y," Roslyn recited in answer, finally understanding the dilemma.

"Ms. Wylie?" Trina asked cautiously.

"Yes," both Alison and Roslyn responded at the same time.

Trina hated to give bad news, but from what she could see, she wasn't the only one who had messed up today. "Ms. Alison. Actually, it looks like your final payment was declined? So, there's your half off right there." Trina tried to make lemonade out of lemons.

Alison flushed hotly with embarrassment. "I... my school payment must have... I..." Alison trailed off. She felt her face heating and knew she was the color of a tomato with purple hair, thanks to her fair skin tone.

Roslyn felt terrible for the woman. She'd been

there before; who hadn't? "We'll take the deal, Trina. Thank you so much for your time. Can we have the code for the lockbox?" Roslyn requested immediately. She didn't want to give Alison too much time to protest again.

"No need," Orion piped up. Alison and Roslyn glanced over at the small boy in surprise. Orion held up his tinker case and a key. "I hacked it."

Alison looked at Roslyn with shock on her face. Roslyn sighed dramatically.

"He what?" Trina shrieked.

"Never mind. Thank you. Bye!" Roslyn quickly said and hung up the phone. "Orion," she turned with a warning in her voice. She didn't admonish him too hard; it was kind of funny, though she didn't laugh. No sense in her encouraging the breaking and entering, even if they hadn't entered yet.

Looking amused, Alison followed Roslyn as she turned and headed toward the cottage with her young son in tow and the luggage she'd unloaded from her vehicle.

Alison dragged her suitcase and a handle bag behind Roslyn, who carried two suitcases and a cloth bag to the cottage. "Orion like the festival?" Alison asked Roslyn to make conversation. Alison felt a need to know more about the woman if they would be sharing a space.

Roslyn turned to look back over her shoulder, her face a careful mask of blankness. "My husband is Miles Thomas." A surprised look passed across Alison's face at the news. "He named the festival after Orion."

Orion led the pack of kids towards the cottage; he carried the key and his tinker case and marched like he was on a mission. Griffin and Taylor packed their suitcases along with them. Taylor had her camera strapped to her shoulder, and Griffin clutched his magazine and portfolio. Both twins were curious about the kid.

"I'm not competing, by the way," Orion announced in a matter-of-fact tone.

Griffin shared a look with his sister. "Well, the competition is for teen poets," Griffin stated, confused.

Orion kept walking but replied with an even tone. "I'm older than I look." The way he said it let the twins know that his age might be a sore subject with the boy on what he could and couldn't do.

Taylor gave a knowing and amused look to Griffin. "How old are you, Orion?" she asked conversationally.

Orion was halfway across the deck by the time Taylor and Griffin reached the stairs. He paused to look at the twins. "Two thousand nine hundred twenty-two days," Orion told them with a straight face.

Taylor did some quick calculations. "Eight years. Exactly eight years?"

"Minus twenty-one," Orion added matter of factly.

Taylor set down her suitcase and smiled, charmed by the boy.

Griffin stepped up next to her with an impressed look on his face. "How'd you do that math so fast?" Griffin wondered.

Taylor grinned. "Turn on your left brain, bro." Taylor shoved him playfully and rolled her eyes. "Poets."

Orion turned back to them. "Taylor. Come on!"

Taylor smiled at the kid and picked up her bag, prepared to follow him.

"How'd he—" Griffin started.

Taylor lifted her suitcase higher and showed her luggage tag with her name on it. "It's on my bag." Taylor followed Orion, and Griffin trailed after them, still looking impressed.

Orion stood at the front door with the key and his tinker case, waiting for Taylor and Griffin to join him. He wore a patient expression on his young face, and every so often, he pushed his glasses back up his nose. He didn't know why the teens took so long; they didn't have that far to go.

"I'm Griffin," Griffin introduced himself as he stepped up to the cottage behind Taylor.

"I know," Orion replied casually with a shrug of his shoulders.

Griffin caught on quicker this time and looked down at his bag to see a luggage tag hanging, and he grinned back at Orion. He found himself to be calmer than he thought he would after the mix-up with the reservations.

"I like your pancake, Griffin," Orion complimented Griffin's beret sincerely.

Taylor slapped a hand to her mouth, hiding the guffaw that had been about to explode out of her. She shot an amused look at her brother. Orion was one precocious child.

"Thank you, Orion." Griffin straightened his beret. It was his lucky beret, and he was rather proud of it. He never went anywhere without it.

"All the best poets wear pancakes," Orion went on before unlocking the door. He said it like it was something that everyone should already know.

Orion stepped into the cottage with his two new friends behind him. It was his first time being here, and he took a moment to look around him and familiarize himself with the space. Once he spotted the loft, he took off running with delight. Lofts were his favorite. The rest of the cottage could wait.

Taylor and Griffin shared another look as they stood at the front door, watching Orion's glee after he saw the loft area.

"Home away from home," Taylor said fondly, glancing around quickly and noting some of the more obvious changes that had gotten made.

"One last time," Griffin reminded her. He loved coming here to this place to do the competition.

"Bittersweet," she replied with a melancholy tone. Taylor didn't dare go further than that and risk upsetting Griffin's sensitive soul.

"Yeah," Griffin agreed sadly. He would miss coming here.

Taylor touched his shoulder, understanding the way it affected her brother. As twins, they were naturally close and often didn't need words to convey their feelings. It was instinctual, something felt but not easily explained, more than a look, more than a tone.

On the heels of the twins, Roslyn and Alison entered the cottage. Roslyn took a look around, much in the manner that her son had moments earlier. It would be home for the next week; she'd better familiarize herself with the place. However, she didn't have the same reaction to the loft that Orion had.

"Mommy!" Orion shouted from the loft.

Everyone turned and looked up at Orion, unsure if they should be concerned or not. Roslyn saw him sitting on the floor with his tinker case beside him, holding on to the railing. The broad smile on his face eased her concern.

"Me and Taylor and Griffin will sleep up here. There're three beds!" Orion declared triumphantly. He got up and darted away out of sight, happy to have solved the problem of sleeping arrangements.

The twins looked at each other and shrugged. The thought didn't bother them; they weren't all that worried about where they'd sleep other than in the cottage and not in their car.

"I get the big one cuz it's bouncy!" Orion shouted again. His declaration was immediately followed by the sound of squeaky mattress springs that let them all know he was jumping on the bed.

Taylor and Griffin shrugged in unison, amused, and headed toward the stairs. "Okay," they called out to Orion in agreement. Both were charmed by the disarming young boy that was smarter than his eight years minus twenty-one days.

Alison and Roslyn finally stepped all the way into the cottage. "They've remodeled," Alison said, looking around in confusion, her brow furrowed and creased.

"Shall we explore?" Roslyn wondered aloud; she set down her bags and headed toward the kitchen. Alison shrugged, mimicked the actions, and followed.

My Daddy doesn't let me bounce," Orion called out to Taylor and Griffin as they came up the stairs. He jumped crazily all over the queen-sized bed and made a mess of the blankets.

Taylor paused at the top, but Griffin passed behind her to one of the twin beds. A stack of spare sheets, including a dark blue queen set, are folded and lying on the couch that sat up in the loft, and Taylor took it all in before responding. The sofa and the queen bed were new; interesting setup, she thought. "It seems kinda dangerous," she commented to the bouncing Orion, her attention moved back to the boy.

"It is," Orion agreed readily. He flopped down on the bed and then scurried off across the room to grab his tinker case and brought it back to the bed with him, and opened it.

Taylor walked over to the third bed and put her suitcase at the foot of it. She looked around and kept the camera on her shoulder. She used her artistic eye and looked for ways she could film to make her documentary. After all, it was their last stay here. There might be something worth the addition to the film up here.

Orion sat on the bed with his tinker case opened in front of him. He didn't look over at Taylor but spoke to her anyway. "Taylor. Is that an old-time movie camera?"

Taylor smiled at the unusual boy and moved to sit on the edge of the bed Orion claimed as his own. "Yeah. I wanna be a filmmaker when I'm older," she explained to the youngster.

Orion still didn't look at Taylor. He continued to tinker with a gizmo in his case. "I wanna be an inventor. I kinda am already," he boasted.

Taylor smiled; she already had formed an attachment to Orion, which wasn't usual for her. She found him endearing. "Me, too. Kinda."

Griffin was stretched out on his bed, reading his magazine with his portfolio nearby. "She's being modest," he told Orion and ratted his sister out. "She's won two festivals already."

Griffin's comment finally had Orion looking up from his tinker case and over at Taylor. He was impressed. He didn't know anyone else that had done that.

"They were small festivals," Taylor responded humbly.

"There're no small festivals," Griffin argued with a matter-of-fact tone. He didn't look up from the magazine he'd read countless times already. "Only small filmmakers."

Orion glanced over at Taylor to see her looking at her brother. Her head was cocked to the side, a slight frown on her face. It interested him to watch the interplay between them; they were the first twins he'd met. He was observant and curious by nature; it was how he learned.

"Then I'm a small filmmaker," Taylor responded unperturbed. "But someday... I'll be big," Taylor vowed. She wasn't afraid to go after her dreams, and she would work hard for them, too.

Orion looked back over at Griffin. "Have you ever won a festival, Griffin?" Orion asked out of curiosity, not trying to put the other teen on the spot. It was pure interest and trying to get to know them both that prompted the question.

Griffin closed his magazine with a swift movement. "Nope." He sat up and looked squarely at Orion. "The Orion Competition is the only one I've ever entered." Griffin grabbed the Beat Poet Magazine and pointed to the cover. "And this is my last chance to beat this guy." He tapped the picture of Dax Linn somewhat aggressively.

Orion listened raptly to Griffin talking. He watched as Taylor got up and walked over to her brother as a show of support. Her being near Griffin seemed to calm him, Orion noted.

"Dax Linn. He's won the last three years," Griffin explained.

Taylor sat down on the edge of Griffin's bed and took the magazine from him. She'd never really looked through it before, only glanced at things Griffin had pointed out when they talked.

"Dax never writes his poems beforehand. He just takes the mic and… boom! He has this way of tapping into the zeitgeist," Griffin praised with wide eyes and a respectful tone.

"Griffin," Taylor interrupted the speech. "Orion doesn't understand that—"

"Sure I do," Orion argued. He held up his phone. "I have Google."

Griffin chuckled a little and smiled at Orion. Taylor opened the magazine to the 'centerfold' and turned it sideways to take a gander at this fantastic poet Griffin couldn't stop talking about lately.

"Oh my," Taylor sighed dreamily. She ran an appreciative eye over the image.

"Yeah. He's hot," Griffin stated agreeably and nodded his head.

"Griffin," Orion called to get his attention. He waited until Griffin looked over at him. "Do you want to be him or be his boyfriend?" Orion asked with a grin.

"Oh!" Taylor exclaimed in surprise. The question seriously amused her, and it was a valid question given Griffin's tone. Her brother only smirked in response.

"From the mouths of babes," Taylor quipped with a smile.

"I'm not a babe," Orion protested vehemently; the statement resulted in the smile disappearing from his face.

Taylor smiled at Orion and saw her brother smile as well. "Sure you are. An almost-eight babe."

Orion liked that statement and giggled to himself a little bit as he turned his attention back to his tinker case. Enough talking; he had work to do.

Chapter Three

Alison and Roslyn peered down the stairs in confusion and concern. Things weren't as advertised or as Alison remembered them to be. Someone had changed everything about the cottage, and it had lost some of its charm in the process.

"I hope the 'system' didn't make another mistake," Roslyn stated using air quotes. None of the pictures she had seen resembled anything she looked at now. The basement looked creepy and like somewhere a monster would live.

The women avoided the stairs and walked across the hall, where Alison paused. "That used to be the master bedroom," she stated from memory. It had been cozy and romantic at one point. Instead, now a hand-written sign hung on the locked door. It read: eBnB Storage Only.

Roslyn tried the knob and suspected it was locked. "Locked," Roslyn confirmed and rattled the knob to prove her statement true.

Alison moved to stand behind her, wondering

why the changes had occurred. It had been laid out so well before, and now it felt clunky. They turned to look out into the house. Nothing was visible except darkness and the door to a utility closet filled with various towels and cleansers.

Alison closed the closet door after she opened it to see what was in that one. "Oh boy."

Taylor stared down at the Beat Poet Magazine centerfold of Dax Linn and looked with a critical eye. "He may be hot…" she trailed off. She straightened the magazine and turned the page. Griffin smiled at Orion but turned to his sister when she spoke. "But you're a better poet. You've really grown this year."

"We'll see," Griffin shrugged, but hope blossomed in his chest at the praise. His sister and mom were the best support a person could ask for, and he was so grateful they were on his side.

Orion switched his attention back to tinkering with his tinker case again. "Daddy says in art, there is no competition."

Taylor and Griffin shared a quizzical look. "And yet…" Taylor began and looked at the magazine pointedly.

"He runs a poetry competition," Griffin finished his sister's sentence. He knew where Taylor had been headed with her statement. It was obvious.

Orion focused on his inventions, his gaze intent. "He's a complicated man," Orion defended his dad, but not with an offended tone.

Griffin broke out a delighted smile at the younger boy and watched him tinker around with something he'd pulled from his case. He had a confidence that amazed

Griffin, and he certainly knew his way around the gadgets in his case.

Taylor found something in the magazine's pages she'd begun to flip through and got a pleased smile on her face. She tapped the page and turned to her brother. "Griffin!" She waited until Griffin looked at her. "You didn't tell me you got featured!" Taylor held the magazine up to the page that Griffin was on.

"Featured is when you get the cover," Griffin pointed out, his tone a little acidic. He motioned to the page. "I got mentioned." The section that spoke of Griffin was a point of contention to him. It felt false and like the magazine was trying to make a point to some of its readers.

Taylor dropped the magazine to the bed between them, not clear why Griffin's expression was one of upset. "A mention is great!" She crowed enthusiastically. "It's an honor to be mentioned!"

"Like it's an honor to be nominated?" He replied sarcastically, making Taylor frown. Griffin wasn't usually so down on himself. There had to be something else behind his reaction.

Roslyn and Alison both wore perplexed expressions as they opened a bathroom door. They peered in and saw a shower stall and not much else. It was clean, at least.

"Two bathrooms is nice," Alison said, trying to remain positive. Almost nothing about the cottage was the same as she remembered, and it felt like a letdown to her.

"I'm not sleeping in a tub," Roslyn stated. Her tone wasn't happy, but it also wasn't unhappy. It was what it was, which was something she abhorred saying. She walked out to continue their exploration of the cottage.

Roslyn emerged from the bottom floor into the stairwell. Alison trailed after her, curious about the other woman. "Will... Miles be joining us?" she wondered curiously. Roslyn halted her forward motion but didn't turn. "I think Griffin might lose his mind," Alison added as a qualifier since she knew how much Griffin admired the man.

Roslyn turned back toward Alison and managed a tight smile. "We're divorced," she said in a clipped tone. Roslyn wasn't trying to take her frustration out on Alison; it just came out that way. Miles was a subject she hadn't come to terms with yet, and it showed when someone mentioned him to her.

"Oh. I—" Alison stuttered out. Roslyn's expression had belied many emotions that Alison understood intimately, and she hadn't intended to bring it out like that. It was just when Roslyn had mentioned Miles she had called him her husband, not an ex.

"Miles didn't want to make a big deal about it," Roslyn tried to explain. She knew it came out badly. "We... didn't want it to be."

"I'm sorry, Roslyn," Alison murmured apologetically. She silently cursed herself for being nosy and insensitive to the woman who went out of her way to make an awkward situation work for all of them.

"Don't be. I'm..." Roslyn trailed off and turned away from Alison. She paused a moment before heading up the stairs. She didn't know what to say, so she stuck to the blunt truth of the matter. "I'm happier now."

Alison watched after her for a long moment. *Will I*

feel the same way someday? Alison wondered to herself. If she were honest, she would say that she mostly was on that side of the coin already; it was just hard to admit. She looked down, then back up and followed Roslyn.

"Is that the utility closet?" Roslyn asked after Alison joined her, pointing to a door.

"It used to be where they stored the deck furniture," Alison mused in confusion at all the changes. What had been the owner's purpose? The space had been entirely functional before and had a homey feel.

"Charming," Roslyn said blandly. She opened the door with Alison standing beside her. Alison looked uncomfortable, and Roslyn cocked an eyebrow. "Really?" she asked snarkily. If she hadn't felt the pull to get to know Alison, she would have been on the phone with the agent again, demanding a resolution.

The room that used to store furniture that Roslyn thought was a utility closet contained a simple bedroom with one double bed—it was not what either of them had expected. Utilitarian in style but impractical for two strangers that were expected to share a living space.

"Okay," Alison stated with hesitation. She reached into her pocket and pulled her cell phone out, dialing a number. "This is stupid. Refund or not—"

"Partial refund," Roslyn reminded her, interrupting.

"Exactly," Alison grumbled. It was unacceptable. She'd figure out something to tell Griffin, some way that she could spin it, so he didn't panic. "The twins and I will find something else, Roslyn. This is just—"

"I don't mind sharing," Roslyn broke in again. Her voice had softened, and her face held a trace of vulnerability.

Alison stared at the other woman, stunned. She stopped dialing and opened her mouth to argue, but no words emerged. Alison was confused and startled by the attempt to help her and the twins. She hadn't even thought about how it would affect Roslyn or Orion. She'd been stuck on her own family.

Roslyn smiled a little at the apparent shock. She'd grown a thicker skin over the past few years, but still, the expression on Alison's face hurt in the way it made Roslyn think she lacked in some manner. Was she so appalling that she couldn't share a bed platonically to sleep?

"Am I so shocking?" Roslyn couldn't help but ask, the self-doubt creeping in. The vulnerable parts of her heart were exposed to condemnation before it even happened.

"Yes," Alison answered without thinking; because they were virtual strangers. "No!" she immediately corrected herself, realizing the mistake she'd made the moment the words left her mouth. Alison hadn't intended it to be an insult, and she felt like a heel.

Roslyn's face flashed with disappointment and hurt. She should have been used to that, but she wasn't. She laughed derisively and walked out of the room. "It's okay," came her parting shot. Roslyn did her best to wall it up inside and move past it.

"I mean... we just met!" Alison called out, wishing she could take the words back. That single moment was all it took Alison to realize that the tough-as-nails appearance and attitude hid some dangerously soft places that would be easy to hurt. Everyone has those spots, Alison reminded herself. Be kind.

"Right," Roslyn answered from the hallway. Her

tone conveyed the conviction that wasn't present. Life is full of disappointment, Roslyn told herself.

Alison called out again as Roslyn continued to retreat. "Roslyn."

"I'll take the couch." Roslyn walked out of sight with her back straight. She didn't look back.

Alison exhaled, feeling awful. She hadn't meant to hurt the woman's feelings. She just found it hard to believe that someone that didn't know her would offer to be so open and kind with someone she didn't know. Alison leaned against the doorframe and shot a look over at the double bed. *Why is everything so damn hard today?!* Alison wondered.

Griffin stood up from the bed and walked to the railing, looking out the high windows. Taylor's comment had gotten to him, and he needed space. Griffin didn't mean to be abrupt or rude. He was already overwhelmed and nervous, and if he overthought that article, it would make it worse.

"Griffin! Come on!" Taylor pleaded with her brother. She got up and stood next to him at the railing. "I'm proud of you." She touched his hand that clutched at the rail.

Frustrated, Griffin swung to face his sister. He wasn't mad; he was hurt. Griffin wasn't used to his twin not understanding his feelings when they usually were in sync. He felt like he shouldn't have to explain himself if she'd read what they wrote. "Beat Poet pulled out four of us who have competed for five years or more. To introduce me, they mentioned our parents."

Taylor suddenly got it. The magazine mentioned that Griffin had lesbian parents, differentiating him from the other competing poets. A ploy, possibly, to engage the readers from that demographic. They hadn't mentioned his talent, only his parents.

"That's what sets me apart," Griffin grumbled, his feelings over the matter still raw since he first noticed it. He was embarrassed by the magazine's choice. "Nothing I've accomplished. Second place three years in a row. Third place the three years before that. I wanna stand out on my own merit. And…" Griffin lowered his voice after he glanced at Orion, "what if they get divorced? Then I don't even have them."

"Griffin," Taylor reached for him. Her heart bled for the pain in her brother's voice. She saw Orion look over at them, listening. "They'll still be our parents." She hesitated before continuing because she never lied to her brother. "And… I don't think it's an 'if.'" Taylor had seen the writing on the wall regarding her moms.

"Anybody want dinner up there?" Alison's voice carried up to the loft.

"Coming!" Griffin shouted back immediately and headed down the stairs, grateful for the reprieve and excuse not to have that conversation. The thought disturbed him.

Taylor started to follow and then paused, looking back at Orion. "I'm sure we brought enough for you, Orion. Our mom is studying to be a chef. She's a really good cook." Taylor wanted him to join them.

Orion smiled back politely. "No, thank you. I have nuggets in my tinker case."

Taylor automatically smiled back at the sweet boy. "Okay." Disappointed but understanding that it might feel awkward for him, she went down to eat dinner.

Orion ate a nugget from his tinker case and looked over at the discarded magazine on Griffin's bed. He casually walked over to the stairs and looked down to ensure everyone was ensconced in the kitchen. Then he moved over to Griffin's bed and studied the magazine.

Orion thumbed through the magazine's pages he picked up and saw the folded-over page that talked about Griffin and three other poets. He looked at the photo of Griffin then read the part that mentioned him. He desperately wanted to know what had turned him from sunny and friendly to sullen and upset.

Orion learned that Griffin and Taylor had two moms, and he smiled because he knew his mom is gay. The twins having two moms made Orion feel like they had something in common, and he loved that fact. He glanced back at the stairs with a smile on his face; his young mind worked overtime to see if he could find a way a bond them further.

Under a beautiful moon in the night sky, the icy river reflected the watery image to the heavens; the five cottage guests all slept in their designated spots inside their shared cottage. Well, most of them slept.

Taylor fell asleep on her side with her Super 8 camera facing her but not recording. She didn't want to know if she snored or drooled. Some things were better left a mystery.

Griffin was on his stomach with his portfolio and pen beside him for those random moments when inspiration struck, which they did, often at two o'clock in the morning after something hit him in a dream and he had to write it down.

Orion lay on his back with an alarm clock robot in his hand and his tinker case still opened next to him. He'd fallen asleep while he worked on his invention.

Roslyn lay on the couch with her pillow, a sheet and blanket, and her eyes wide open. Her brain moved at the speed of light where she went over everything that happened during the day, how screwed up it was, and her part in it all. There were moments she could have handled better.

She shoved the blanket off her and swung her pajama-clad legs off the couch. Sleep wasn't happening, she thought as she let out a dramatic sigh. Roslyn sat up and stood to walk into the kitchen. Maybe a drink of water would help, or a light snack. It was worth a shot.

No one else was in the kitchen, and Roslyn crossed to the cupboards. She opened one quietly, then another, until she found the glasses. Roslyn selected one and went to the sink and filled it with water; she drank it down and filled it again. Carrying it with her, Roslyn returned to the couch, not hungry after all, and sat there in silence. *Maybe it was too silent,* Roslyn thought.

"You can't do this. It's his last year!" Alison cried out from the bedroom, breaking the quiet atmosphere.

Roslyn paused at the upset tone Alison used. She didn't sound angry; it was more of a badly hurt tone. She turned toward the hallway and listened; her brows creased in concern, not to mention curiosity.

"With everything going on, he really needs to know you're still there for him," Alison burst out. "Of course, he's affected!" Alison argued with whoever she spoke to on the phone.

Roslyn bowed her head and closed her eyes. It was almost too painful to listen to, and she understood well, knowing now that it was a relationship issue. It also told Roslyn part of what she'd wondered, if Alison was involved with someone or not.

"Please, Jac. Not for me, for him. Please be there," Alison pleaded with so much emotion in her voice it was all Roslyn could do not to cry.

With her eyes filled with unshed tears, she headed back to the living room to lay back on the couch. If she stayed closer, she'd be tempted to rush in and console Alison, letting the other woman know that Roslyn had eavesdropped on her conversation with Jack.

Alison sat cross-legged on the bed in her pajamas. There's only one pillow, and it wasn't one that she wanted to hug; she'd rather it be someone she loved. She hung up the phone and slowly lowered it, letting it drop from her fingers onto the bed she would sleep in alone.

Alison stared at the phone for a moment, then looked up and toward the rest of the house. The expression on her face was unreadable—she's perfected that—but easy enough to see that she was in emotional turmoil if anyone cared to look. Alison assumed that no one would look, so she let the vulnerability and pain show for only a brief second; that was all she would allow.

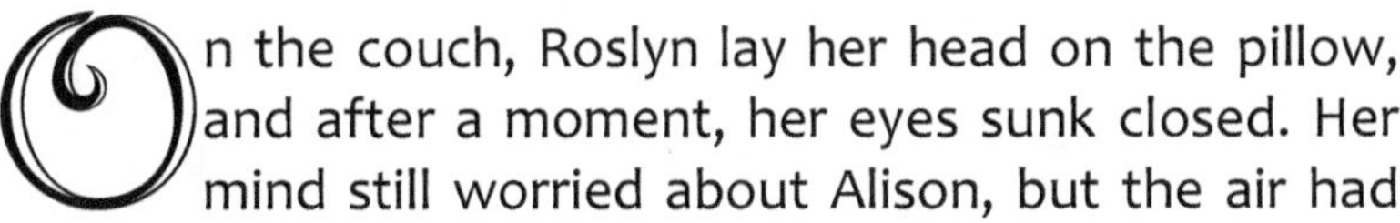

On the couch, Roslyn lay her head on the pillow, and after a moment, her eyes sunk closed. Her mind still worried about Alison, but the air had become heavy with sadness, and all too familiar with that feeling, Roslyn slept.

Chapter Four

Day 2

The shallow crystal-clear water of the river flowed over the rocks that lined the riverbed as the sun rose to kiss the sky in a brilliant display of color. Wildlife drank from the cool flowing water and nibbled on the greenery that covered the banks. Soon they wouldn't be able to; it would be buried in snow.

Nestled inside the cottage, Orion and Taylor were still sound asleep. But not Griffin. He sat up in his bed, his pajamas still on, and read from his portfolio. His mouth moved with the words, and he looked up often since he had the poem pretty much memorized. He'd been practicing the prose he would recite for the competition in the preliminary round.

He'd titled the poem 'Just Words.' He underlined twice the notation that read: For the preliminaries. However, it wasn't likely he would forget. How could he? The competition was all he'd thought about for the past few months, and now it was here.

Words. It's just words.
Repeated over and over.
Sticks and stones and words.

But words have power.
The confession of the ages.
The secret of society.
Sticks and stone and words.

Beyond pheromones.
Beyond commonalities.
It's the way we speak
the words we choose
that build up or tear down
everything and everyone.
Push me away. Descend.
Draw me near. Ascend.

In language lies the strength
to rend or render friendship.
To rend or render love.
To rend or render family.
Sticks and stones and words.

My victory is meaningless
unless I bring you with me.
We rise or fall together.

Griffin looked out into the middle of somewhere inside his mind as he practiced. He kept trying to visualize an audience in front of him. He shook his head, unhappy and frustrated with himself, and started again, his voice quiet in the room.

Words. It's just words.
Repeated over and over.
Sticks and stones and words.

The couch was empty in the living room, and the sheet and blanket were folded and neatly stacked on the pillow. There was no sign of Roslyn as Alison came out of the bedroom and moved through the living room to the kitchen. It was like she hadn't been there at all. Then she noticed the other woman out on the deck staring out at the view; not that she blamed her for that, Alison did that often too.

Alison paused to study Roslyn. She felt awful about their last conversation and the way she blurted out her misgivings. After a few moments of rudely staring while trying to figure the woman out, Alison returned her gaze to the ground and continued on her way to the kitchen. She'd been doing that a lot, looking down instead of her usual meet the world head-on look. Alison supposed it was from the way her relationship with Jac had gone. She admired Roslyn's tenacity and bold strength—Alison could use a bit of that right now.

Roslyn stood at the railing and took in the scenery. It was stunning and so calm—a nice contrast to her chaotic thoughts and emotions. For example, the negative thoughts that had her gripping the railing so tight that it left her knuckles white. She needed to get out of her own head. Nothing good would come of this mindset. She'd been down this road before more than once.

She took a deep breath in and refocused her attention on the rugged natural beauty this place offered and soaked it in. The crisp, clean wintry air filled her lungs, and she whooshed it out slowly. *Wash, rinse, and repeat,* Roslyn told herself and took in another lungful of cold air. She kept doing that until she felt her pulse slow down.

Alison scooped the coffee grounds into the French Press while the kettle heated up and whistled its morning song. She moved in an autopilot fashion, removed the pot from the stove, depressed the French Press, and prepared two cups of coffee. She hoped that Roslyn liked coffee; she wasn't sure what else to do as a peace offering.

At Alison's last glance, Roslyn still stood outside at the railing, so she gently opened the back door when the coffee was finished and stepped out carrying the steaming mugs. It didn't even seem like the other woman was present until she let out a heavy sigh and turned. They each stared at the other for a moment, trying to read expressions and body language.

Alison's overall goal was to make it up to Roslyn after last night's conversation. She didn't know that Roslyn overheard her conversation with Jac; the thought that someone could overhear her didn't even cross her mind. Alison just felt nervous and apologetic about the whole thing and wanted to smooth it over, so Roslyn's piercing gaze and expression were lost on Alison.

"Good morning," Roslyn finally said, her tone somewhat distracted.

"I made coffee," Alison smiled and held out a cup.

Roslyn took it slowly and glanced at the wedding ring on Alison's finger. She felt bad for whatever the woman was going through with her husband, Jack. She knew it wasn't an easy road to traverse from her own experience.

"It's Moroccan," Alison offered. "There's cardamom, nutmeg, ginger, black pepper, and cloves."

Roslyn looked down at the cup and inhaled the spicy aroma. "I haven't had coffee in ten years," Roslyn responded finally.

Feeling defeated, Alison tried to school her expression. "Oh."

The tone and crestfallen look didn't get past Roslyn's notice. "Miles hated the smell." Roslyn drank the hot liquid slowly, groaned, and saw a small smile tease Alison's lips. "This is incredible."

"Thank you." Relief washed through Alison as she realized her peace offering didn't get rejected. She stepped forward to the railing and looked out at the incredible view she looked forward to coming to in the wintertime. It was because of the grace of this woman that it was possible this year.

Roslyn stood by her side as they drank their coffee, admiring the view of the river and trees. "It really is beautiful here," Roslyn sighed. It felt comfortable to be here like this, standing next to the mostly perfect stranger of a woman. It had been years since she had felt this relaxed around someone.

"We only come in December for the competition," Alison told her, sipping on her coffee. "But I imagine the river is amazing in the summertime."

Roslyn turned to face Alison, propping her hip against the railing. "No polar bear plunge?" she asked with a straight face.

Alison laughed delightedly and mock-shivered. "The waters like forty degrees."

Roslyn lifted her mug to take another drink but paused. "Last night, I—" she began but was interrupted by the ringing of her phone. She worked on fishing the phone out of her pocket and lifted it to see who was calling.

"I'll make breakfast," Alison said to give Roslyn a moment of privacy for her phone call.

"No, no," Roslyn protested, not wanting Alison to leave. "I'll take us all out. This'll be fast. It's Willy Patterson."

Alison's jaw dropped open in surprise. Will Patterson was a famous and prolific writer. "The author?" she asked in shock, wondering how Roslyn knew the man.

Roslyn rolled her eyes dramatically. "I guess." She answered the phone and put it on speakerphone for Alison's benefit. "Will. Stop calling me."

Alison looked amused by this, but Roslyn was in an all-business attitude mindset for the phone call from the author. He was on her last nerve, and it was all she could do to remain civil with the man who had interrupted her week off.

"You're my editor!" Willy shouted through the phone.

"And not your friend. I'm away for the week," Roslyn reminded the high-maintenance writer.

"But I need you!" Willy declared hotly.

"So does my son," Roslyn answered in a stern tone. She rolled her eyes again as she talked with the annoying and demanding author. He was lucky she didn't chew him up and spit him out. It was bad enough dealing with him while Roslyn was on the clock, but now in her free time?

"He doesn't have a deadline," Willy replied with a rude and haughty tone.

"Childhood has its own deadline, Will," Roslyn answered firmly.

"God, that's good. Can I use that?" Willy's tone changed instantly.

Alison stifled a laugh when Roslyn motioned to the phone with a gesture that said, *See? This guy is a hack!*

"No. Write your own damn novel," Roslyn stated in a firm voice. None of the friendly tones she used with Alison were present in her voice. She spoke curtly and in a manner that was easy to decipher as irritated.

"I can't! I need you!" Willy whined dramatically like a child who didn't get their way in a candy store.

"I'm back on Tuesday night. Send me pages then," Robyn replied, putting her foot down.

Alison found the conversation funny and was surprised that someone that well known was that needy and whiny. She was also impressed with how Robyn handled him and was unyielding in devoting her time to her son. It showed her to be a good mother; that was something that impressed Alison above her knowing an author.

"Roslyn! No! I'll fail! I'll—" Willy began another tirade.

Roslyn was wholly unmoved by the entire thing and all his antics. "Goodbye, Will," Roslyn interrupted and hung up the phone. "The more famous people I work with, the less faith I have in humanity."

Alison laughed, amused. She shook her head slightly at the adult's immature behavior, especially considering that he needed Roslyn's help.

"Let me take us all out to eat," Roslyn offered

again. She considered the choices in town. She typically defaulted to whatever was fast. "Mcdonald's has those burrito... breakfast things."

Alison grinned. She could definitely do better than fast food. She reached out and kindly touched Roslyn's hand. "Let me cook for you."

Roslyn's face became still. She opened her mouth to say something, argue perhaps, but then closed it. She wasn't sure how to respond to Alison's gesture. She couldn't remember the last time someone cooked a meal for her, much less voluntarily without a bill that accompanied it.

Alison's hand remained on Roslyn's as she held her coffee mug with both hands. Alison's tone was light, friendly, and had humor in it. She finally felt back on stable ground with a mission to perform. "Let me restore your faith in humanity."

Alison turned and headed back into the house with Roslyn watching her go. Once Alison was out of sight, Roslyn tilted her head to the side, tickled at her reaction to Alison's touch. "Please do," Roslyn said quietly and then followed her inside.

Chapter Five

A large stack of fluffy pancakes covered in blueberries and whipped cream sat in front of Orion. He had his fork poised and ready to dive in. It was his second helping, though, from his reaction, you wouldn't know that. His eyes were wide with amazement, and his mouth opened in shock; when he wasn't chewing, that was. A glass of milk sat nearby, ready to wash the fantastic food down.

Roslyn and Alison watched Orion with happy smiles on their faces. Empty plates sat in front of them, and their coffee mugs were filled with the brew Alison had made.

"I think I broke your son," Alison quipped with a grin. Orion's reaction and delight made all the effort worth the work it took.

"I don't cook," Roslyn informed her with a serious look. "At all."

Griffin and Taylor sat at the other end of the table, with Orion next to Griffin. The teens were only halfway through their fruit and pancakes. Griffin ate with a determined look on his face while Taylor smiled at Orion in adoration.

"Orion?" Taylor called out to him. She hated to interrupt his devotion to her mom's cooking, but she wanted to capture the moment.

"Uh," Orion muttered distractedly.

"Can I film you taking your first bite?" she asked the boy. Orion nodded a little. Taylor glanced over at Roslyn as she lifted her camera from the bench next to her. "Is that okay, Roslyn?"

Roslyn nodded her assent, sipped her coffee, and smiled. Alison grinned at her daughter, pleased with the polite questions. There was never a question about how Alison felt about her kids and how talented and fabulous they were.

Like they were in slow motion, Orion moved his fork toward his excellent breakfast and scooped up a forkful of whipped cream to begin as a true movie star would. He ate it up, and his eyes grew even wider. Taylor filmed all Orion's reactions, and Griffin paused his own eating to smile at the boy.

"No nitrous oxide!" Orion exclaimed happily. That led to him digging into his breakfast with gusto. He'd hammed it up as much as his patience would allow. It was time to eat.

Alison gave Roslyn a curious look after Orion's declaration. All Roslyn could do was shake her head in laughter. She loved her intelligent little man. "It's the propellant in Reddi-Wip."

Griffin enjoyed watching Orion wolf down his pancakes. It was fun to see the young boy enjoy something so simple, something he was used to and probably took for granted more than he should. He pseudo-quoted Robert Frost. "Today, you took the road less traveled, and it made all the difference."

"Griffin!" Orion said, startled, talking around a mouthful of food. It was messy and adorable.

"You've got a little... blueberry there, buddy," Griffin pointed to Orion's face. Who cared about table manners when you had someone that excited about food and poetry?

"I know that poem!" Orion stated happily.

Griffin picked up a napkin and attempted to hand it to Orion, but Orion was too focused on his food to notice. "Yeah, pretty much the whole world knows that poem."

Orion was practically bouncing. He was so excited to share the facts he knew about the famous poem. He wasn't pretentious about it, just happy to share his smartness, as his mother called it, even though Orion was confident that wasn't a real word.

"And pretty much the whole world gets it wrong! Frost says right in the poem that the two roads are equal and the same. But, he says, when he talks about them in the future, he says he's gonna say they were different to make it a more interesting poem," Orion informed the twins.

Griffin nodded at the information, smiling wide, and listened attentively.

"He wrote a poem about getting the idea to write a poem!" Orion added as an afterthought.

At the other end of the table, Roslyn flipped her phone over absently on the table. She tried to hide the fact that she was upset, but Alison caught the expression before Roslyn could mask it. The

Road Less Traveled was a poem that meant a great deal to her, and a few years ago, Miles ruined it by deconstructing the poem in front of Orion. When Roslyn's gaze shifted, Alison caught her eye and gave her a questioning look.

Feeling naked, she lowered her voice so only Alison could hear. "Miles... deconstructs poems. Orion loves it," Roslyn explained. Her tone changed to one she used when mimicking her ex-husband. "The Road Less Traveled is actually about assigning false importance to inconsequential details and the human nature of self-deception." Roslyn grimaced and looked down at the table. "Ugh. And I... really love that poem." Roslyn sighed sadly.

Alison watched Roslyn closely. She wore a tough façade, and she wore it well, but it was apparent to Alison that Roslyn was emotionally as vulnerable as Alison herself felt over the mess with Jac. Relationships and love were complicated enough, even when they didn't fail. Scars happened, something Alison was too familiar with in her own life. Roslyn had just let one show, and it was a gift to witness.

Taylor held her camera up as she continued to film, though her head turned to the women at the other end of the table. From where she sat, it appeared as though Roslyn and her mom were attracted to each other. Taylor was slightly amused by what she saw, but something else struck her when she turned her attention back to the boys. *Are the boys bonding? Are all of us bonding?* Taylor wondered. Her heart warmed at the idea.

Griffin faced Orion as they talked about the poem. He smiled and nodded sweetly at the boy, but Orion seemed to catch on to what he was doing and called him on it.

"Wait. Did you already know that?" Orion bluntly asked.

Griffin hesitated to admit it, but he wasn't one to lie either. "Yeah."

"Why didn't you interrupt me?" Orion wondered aloud.

Griffin smiled gently and explained his actions. "I was raised that when someone tries to tell you something new, they're trying to give you a gift. It doesn't hurt anyone to pretend we're hearing something cool for the first time. But it *can* hurt if someone thinks they can never give you anything."

Roslyn glanced over at the boys and half-listened to their conversation. Griffin certainly didn't sound like a typical teenage boy, and that impressed her all around. She looked back at Alison admiringly. "How did you get a teenage boy to talk like that?"

Alison looked fondly down at the chattering boys. "That's not me," she admitted, only a hint of bitterness in her voice. She looked back at Roslyn. "That's all Jac. Master of charm. My... ex." The word hurt to say, but it was beyond time, to be honest with herself about the situation.

The two women stared at each other in understanding, and both realized that they had shared a moment that was raw, thoughtful, and honest. Maybe they even took a step toward healing a part of themselves that would allow new things to begin.

The five new friends all sat around the kitchen table after enjoying the fabulous homemade breakfast. They talked and soaked up each other's company and had a wonderful morning. Outside, the wildlife munching on the fauna could hear the faint sounds of laughter coming from inside the cottage. It didn't bother them; they continued with their meal.

CHAPTER SIX

Five people bustled out of the little cottage and headed towards the silver SUV that belonged to Roslyn. Each bundled up for warmth, and Alison and Roslyn each wore their identical olive-green puffy jackets. If one didn't know better, they looked like a family headed out for some fun.

The three kids climbed into the backseat with Orion in the middle. Taylor had her camera with her, and Griffin carried his portfolio, pen, and magazine. These days, he didn't leave home without it.

Alison opened the passenger side door and got in while Roslyn situated herself behind the wheel. "You sure about this?" Alison asked as Roslyn closed her door. That uncomfortable feeling crept back up inside; she wasn't used to people doing kind things for her with no expectations.

"You cook, I'll drive. It's very progressive," Roslyn stated with a hand flip, seemingly oblivious to the wrongness of the statement.

"That's not progressive at all," Alison protested

with a confused look.

Roslyn nodded. "I heard it as soon as I said it." She dropped the subject and started the car. The kids were all quiet in the backseat, and once they were underway, Roslyn snuck a glance at Alison, unable to help herself.

Alison appeared lost in thought as she watched the road pass by out the window. Something about the woman made her arresting to Roslyn, and if she was honest with herself, Alison looked quite dashing today. There was a healthy glow to her skin, and her outfit complimented her complexion and her figure. Not to mention that when she smiled, Roslyn felt dizzy.

A car driving by honked and drew Roslyn's attention back to the task at hand, which was driving safely into town. Roslyn got lost while she stared at Alison for a moment, and the car drifted into the passing lane. She swiveled her head back to the road and jerked the wheel to correct her drift.

Alison looked ahead in concern, then back at Roslyn with a grin, as if she had known what had distracted her. *What just happened?* Alison thought to herself nervously, wishing she had been the one to drive.

The view coming into Leavenworth was always picturesque. Even more so with the holiday charm in full swing. The little touristy Bavarian old-world town was always fun to roam around and usually had some sort of artistic festival happening. This time of year, it was the Orion Poetry Competition, and tomorrow night was the first stage. The preliminaries that had Griffin so vexed and anxious.

After Roslyn parked near the big gazebo in the

town center, that's where the poetry competition would take place, they all piled out of the SUV and held out their cell phones. All five chimed with overlapping dings of messages.

"Numbers exchanged," Roslyn declared happily. They'd all decided to make sure everyone had the other's numbers stored so that they all knew where each other were and could be reached at any time. It was a mother thing.

"But everyone try to stay together. We have four hours before the reading tonight," Alison suggested in that tone that told you it wasn't really a suggestion even if she used a pleasant voice. It was a mother thing.

Griffin and Taylor wasted no time in making tracks. Orion frowned, and his shoulders sunk. He'd been hoping to spend more time with the twins and do something cool with them. He wasn't used to older siblings, and that's what they had begun to feel like to him.

Alison squatted down next to the downcast boy, and Roslyn followed suit on the other side. "Big kids are jerks sometimes," Alison consoled Orion gently with an empathetic tone.

"But they don't mean to be," Roslyn added in a softened tone from her usual voice. She knew the twins hadn't meant to hurt Orion's feelings and didn't want the blame placed on their heads.

Orion's stiffness eased. "Yeah," he replied drily. "Teens."

Alison grinned. "But you've got your mom and me, and we're way more fun," Alison promised and beamed a bright smile at him.

"Really?" Orion perked up. She had his attention

now.

"Yeah!" Alison stood up and beamed the devastating grin at Roslyn.

"Cuz Mommy has credit cards!" Roslyn threw in for good measure, trying to keep control over her emotions. It was never hard to spoil her child, and she had a sneaking suspicion that Alison never really treated herself.

Alison laughed delightedly, and Orion's smile grew. It was time for some fun to happen! He was more than ready for that.

Griffin carried his portfolio and magazine tucked under his arm and walked down the holiday-decorated street. He chatted, smiled, and laughed with his sister as they looked in various store windows. Every time Griffin caught sight of the Super 8 camera she carried, Griffin smiled a little wider. He loved being able to support her artistic ventures the way she supported his. In that way, he didn't care if she filmed him. It was for art.

A long-armed, plush, clockwork doll sat in the corner, and once Orion spotted it, he reached for the toy in delight. To him, it looked like something he would invent, and it called to him. The rest of the toys in the shop faded into the background. Orion stood there and stared in fascination at the toy. He loved it, and it wasn't even his.

Roslyn simply held up her credit card for the clerk that hovered, who took it from her hand with a smile. It was the easiest sale the clerk would have of the day. The look on Orion's face when he gazed at the doll was priceless, and Roslyn would do anything she could to keep it there. She could afford the extra expense with the way she saved.

When Roslyn, Alison, and Orion walked out of the store, the doll had its arms lovingly wrapped around Orion's neck, like he was giving it a piggyback ride. Alison held his hand on one side and his mom on the other. He was sure this wouldn't have happened if he'd been with Griffin and Taylor. Orion was no longer worried about not having a good time with his mom and Alison. He had fun!

Alison and Roslyn swung Orion between them; his happy squeals rang out as his feet left the ground, and the doll flew out behind him like a cape. Over Orion's head, Alison and Roslyn grinned at each other, their hearts light with Orion's laughter and youthful energy. They didn't see Griffin and Taylor walk out of a different store behind them, talking and laughing, and headed in the other direction. They missed each other by less than a foot.

Alison and Roslyn stopped in front of the delectable chocolate store, and Alison smiled over at Roslyn as she watched Orion bounce up and down in excitement. What kid didn't like chocolate? Roslyn just shook her head at her son's antics and puffed up her cheeks in mock horror because if she went in that store, that's what she would look like the next day. She felt like she could look at chocolate and gain weight. She didn't have Orion's metabolism, that was for sure.

Orion ignored his mother's silent protest and darted past Alison to enter the store. Alison snickered and took Roslyn's hand in hers and pulled her inside the sinful store after her. Roslyn trailed behind, liking the feel of Alison's hand holding hers.

A tantalizing selection of gourmet chocolates in a glass case greeted them, and Orion perched right in front of it, with his new doll peeking over his shoulder. He practically glued his nose to the display case. If Roslyn let him have his way, they'd leave with the entire inventory in their hands, and the kid would never sleep or stop talking.

Roslyn chose for Orion and selected four truffles that he had made noise about wanting, and then added four more to a separate box that she had noticed Alison looking at during their perusal. She handed the boxes to Orion and Alison, and they turned to leave the store before temptation grabbed hold of her more than it already had. She was sure the scent of chocolate alone had added six pounds.

Orion carried his box clutched in his hands and already had one truffle stuffed into his mouth, happily chomping away. Roslyn and Alison trailed behind the overly content boy, and Alison opened her box with a happy sigh, pulled out one truffle, and held it up. Then she looked back into the box as if she wasn't sure which one she really wanted to eat since they all looked delicious.

Without overthinking about it, lest she loses her nerve, Roslyn playfully ate the truffle right out of Alison's fingers. The flirtatious move surprised both women into a moment of stunned silence, but then they both laughed and followed Orion, not wanting him to get too far ahead of them.

Griffin and Taylor crossed the street, headed toward a bookstore they visited each year. Taylor ripped a soft pretzel she'd bought in half and split it with her brother, handing him the larger piece. She bit off a chunk and ate it, savoring the salty dough.

Griffin paused and froze in place once they reached the sidewalk. Directly in his line of sight was a sign that advertised the poetry competition. Nerves took over, and he just stared.

Taylor glanced back, noticing Griffin wasn't next to her, and saw him staring at the sign that sat outside the gazebo announcing the seventh annual Orion Poetry Festival Teen Poetry Competition. It sat on an easel and listed the event times. *Preliminaries on Friday, December 7, at 5:00 PM. Finals on Monday, December 10, at 7:00 PM. Dress Warmly!*

Taylor looked back at her brother, still frozen in place. A gentle smile graced her face, and she tugged on his arm to snap him out of his daze. Taylor didn't want Griffin to get lost inside the nervousness she was certain clouded his brain. She recognized the look on his face. They continued on their way to the bookstore.

Right after that, a horse-drawn carriage rolled up the road carrying Alison, Orion, and Roslyn. All three of them had broad smiles plastered on their wind-kissed rosy faces. Orion leaned against his mother, and Roslyn leaned her head against Orion's in the most adorable way. Alison couldn't help but sneak glances at them lovingly. She missed those days with her kids and was pleased to witness it with her new friend.

The sign on the door declared A Book for All Seasons. It was one of the twin's favorite stores. The door chimed as they opened it and entered. Both Taylor and Griffin paused in front of another easel, this one announcing a special appearance by Miles Thomas at 5:00 PM.

"We're a few hours early for Miles' reading," Taylor commented. She wasn't a massive fan of the man, but her brother looked forward to it, so she was happy enough to join him.

"Let's just get warm, then we'll go find Mom," Griffin suggested. He headed off without his sister to browse the books. He didn't intentionally ignore his sister; he was distracted by the thought of finding a new book to read.

Taylor shrugged and headed in the opposite direction. There were a few things she wanted to look at anyway. Taylor wound her way through the small but charming bookstore, her gaze creating a wish list of things she hoped to purchase one day. Taylor had a passion for all forms of storytelling, and she had her eye on a volume, and she wondered if the bookstore carried it. She browsed, lost in her own world, much in the way Griffin was.

Griffin stood in the poetry section, looking at various volumes. There were several he had found that he wanted. So many books to choose from, and it seemed he could always find ways to grow his to-be-read pile.

"In the poetry section as always," Taylor cajoled him as she walked up after about an hour of doing her own browsing.

"Where else?" Griffin shrugged. He was a creature of habit, and everyone knew it. He knew what he liked. There was nothing wrong with that.

Taylor half-smiled, half-smirked at her brother. "Broaden your horizons. They have a really good selection of indie graphic novels." Taylor motioned absently behind them. She wasn't picking on him; she just liked to poke at him now and then.

Griffin glanced in the direction of the graphic novels to make his sister happy, but he focused intently on the poetry section. Graphic novels were more of his sister's thing. "Yeah. That's cool," he stopped mid-sentence. His eyes had landed on Dax Linn. Griffin froze and blatantly stared. His eyes were as huge as saucers, and his voice a hushed whisper. "Taylor," Griffin called to her, his tone urgent.

"What?" Taylor responded and wondered what was happening to put that look on her brother's face.

"Don't look," Griffin whispered dramatically.

"Don't look where?" Taylor asked and automatically looked around.

"Oh my god, Taylor!" Griffin admonished her. He threw his arm around his sister and huddled them forward as he turned the magazine he'd been carrying everywhere outward. Griffin gestured to the magazine cover, making Taylor smile. "He's here. Dax Linn is... he's..." Griffin stuttered out excitedly.

Taylor straightened up. "Oh," she declared softly, understanding. She snatched the magazine from Griffin's hands. "I'll be right back." Taylor wasn't anywhere near as shy as her unassuming brother was.

"Taylor! No!" Griffin whisper-shouted at her.

Dax was in the process of picking up a graphic

novel titled Teatro di Freak off the shelf and started to flip through it.

"Excuse me," Taylor interrupted Dax, not in the least sorry for it either.

He looked over and looked her up and down. "Hey."

When Dax smiled, Taylor suddenly became a little nervous and momentarily forgot about the magazine she held. Taylor glanced at the graphic novel that Dax had been looking at when she walked up. "That's actually really good. I got it last month," Taylor told him.

Dax flipped through it again, his demeanor relaxed. "So did I. I thought it was cool it was here. It's pretty indie."

Taylor was surprised that he even knew it. "Yeah, it is," she agreed. Dax dazzled her a little.

"I like how it's laid out like a film. Like a storyboard," Dax explained his thoughts and carried on the conversation.

"Not unexpected. Comics and films. They're both visual mediums," Taylor replied, enjoying the topic of conversation.

Dax thought about what Taylor said, then added another thought. "True. But that's like saying a poet and a novelist are the same because they both use words."

Despite her intentions not to fall for the charm, Taylor felt inexplicably drawn into the conversation. *Damn it!* she thought. *Is he hot and smart?!* As Dax stared at her, waiting for a response to his comparison, Taylor suddenly remembered the magazine she held, and she slapped him in the chest with it. "Will you sign this?"

"Sure," Dax smiled enticingly. He lifted his pen and clicked it as if it were magic.

Griffin watched the encounter while he hid behind the book display of poetry. He was simultaneously excited and jealous that he wasn't the one talking to the famous teen poet. Sometimes his twin had more gumption than he did.

Dax signed the magazine and handed it back with a slight smirk. Taylor grabbed it and turned, walking away. "You're welcome," he called to her retreating form, smiling. He stood there and watched her, knowing he'd made an impression.

"Thank you!" Taylor replied without looking back. She was attracted but still had reservations.

Griffin straightened and bounced with excitement as Taylor approached with the signed magazine. She held out the autographed magazine with no fanfare, just a simple gesture.

"Merry Christmas," Taylor told her brother.

"Oh my god... oh my god... oh my god!" Griffin chanted and clutched the magazine to his chest. Elated would be an understatement. He'd idolized Dax Linn for a while now.

Taylor stifled a laugh. "Let's get you some fresh air," she suggested. Taylor led him out of the store. She glanced back at Dax once and smiled a little before following her brother out the door. A bit of flirting never hurt anyone.

Griffin stood out on the sidewalk staring at his magazine with reverent joy on his face. Taylor let the bookstore door close all the way behind her and joined her brother.

"I need to go sit down," Griffin declared and walked off abruptly, feeling overwhelmed.

"See you at five!" Taylor shouted to him. She

shook her head a little at his excitement and headed in the opposite direction to do her own thing. She wanted to check out more stores before they all met up at the bookstore that night.

Chapter Seven

Alison and Roslyn walked down the sidewalks of Leavenworth, window shopped, and trailed after Orion as he wandered, a little amped up after he devoured his chocolate.

"I can't believe you've never explored Leavenworth before," Alison told Roslyn as she led her around the town.

"Uh... it's cold!" Roslyn joked. Alison laughed good-naturedly. The moment was lost when Roslyn tensed up after seeing her ex-husband walking toward them with his usual confident swagger.

"Orion!" Miles shouted. He dropped to one knee and held his arms open for Orion to charge into them. He wasn't play-acting for Roslyn's benefit; he truly did love his son. Divorce didn't change that.

Orion stopped in his tracks; his sweet face lit up enough to rival the holiday lights. "Daddy!" Orion screeched. "See you at the bookstore, Mommy!"

Orion took off at a dead run to his father. His new doll hung around his neck and flew out behind him. Miles scooped up the boy lovingly and nuzzled him affectionately.

Alison smiled at the touching reunion of father and child. It warmed her heart to see open affection like that. However, she noticed the pained expression on Roslyn's face and was surprised when the woman turned away abruptly and walked in the opposite direction. Alison waited a moment, then hurried to follow. Orion was in good hands, but Roslyn needed some attention now.

Roslyn had an excellent-paced, brisk walk, and it took a minute for Alison to catch up with the woman. "Where are we going?" Alison asked a little breathlessly. She tried to match the taller woman's longer stride, but it felt like a jog to Alison.

"Away from my ex-husband," Roslyn snapped, not slowing her pace at all.

Then it made sense to Alison, the expression, the need to get away. Roslyn was hurting and didn't want it to show. Alison guessed the split wasn't a very amicable one. Wanting to help, she moved quickly, stepped in front of Roslyn, and stopped her momentum with a hand on her arm. "Hey." She did her best to take Roslyn's mind off her ex. "Are you hungry?"

Roslyn wanted to be polite, but the sight of her ex-husband did a number on her and screwed up her mind. She had expected some reaction; she knew she hadn't dealt with the emotional fallout from the divorce yet. Maybe it was that she expected him to address her, and he hadn't. His focus had been solely on Orion. She hadn't even talked to *him*, and she felt this way, hurt, angry, and sad. Finally, she exhaled and admitted, "I'm starving." She couldn't dwell on this, not now.

Alison reached out to take Roslyn's hand in hers, the woman's emotions palpable, and began to lead her away. "Come with me." Alison crossed the street holding Roslyn's hand. It was time to be there for Roslyn, and in doing so, it took her mind off her issues with Jac.

At The Christmas Shop, an incredible decorated tree was on display. Perfectly placed ribbon, gold and silver balls, quaint little decorations, and even some snowflakes perched and hung on the branches. It was a stunning piece of art. Taylor had her camera at the ready and lifted it, clicking it on. She turned in a circle and captured the tree, then panned across the store and filmed all the details so elaborately displayed. Once she finished, she lowered the camera and flashed a brilliant smile at all the people that looked at her with curiosity and wondered what she was doing.

At The Sausage Garden, Alison and Roslyn stood under the signage outside the front door. The spiced aroma drifted out the door that opened and closed as people entered and exited. "This place is my favorite," Alison told Roslyn, who looked skeptical. Alison's stomach rumbled in expectation.

"Sausage?" Roslyn questioned. She made a face that showed her uncertainty with Alison's decision. "Not really my thing."

Alison assumed Roslyn was making a penis joke and laughed. "Ha-ha."

"What?" Roslyn wrinkled her face in confusion, not getting it. The scents that wafted out on the air smelled good; Roslyn just wasn't a fan of sausage.

"Just trust me. These are amazing," Alison

promised with a tug on Roslyn's arm. She walked into the restaurant, and Roslyn hesitatingly followed. Alison was working toward being a chef, so she hoped that the woman knew what she was talking about—it was worth a try.

Griffin gazed up at the wooden gazebo. His nerves kicked into high gear as a flashback overcame him of years past when he stood on that platform. *Holding a wireless microphone and his portfolio, Griffin stood on the stage, his breath coming in rapid bursts of steam puffing from his lips. He stepped forward nervously toward the gazebo's railing out to the large crowd gathered made up of family and friends of the competitors. He supposed there were others there too.*

The gazebo was empty now, though; the large park surrounding had started to fill with people milling around, but not a real crowd, per se. Enough to put Griffin into the mindset that he was being watched and judged. That was what triggered the anxiety and the flashbacks.

Griffin took a deep breath and tried to calm himself down, centering himself in the moment. The here and now, instead of in the past. He looked down and smiled a little. *I can do this!* he told himself with an internal pep talk.

The sound of familiar laughter had Griffin looking toward the noise and saw Alison and Roslyn walking down the sidewalk, each eating a sausage from the place that Alison loved, and they ate at every time they came here.

"You know... it's vegetarian," Griffin heard Alison tell Roslyn. She must have thought it was meat, Griffin surmised.

Roslyn stopped dead in her tracks. She had just finished her sausage. "Shut up!" Roslyn cried.

"Really. Good vegetarian food has to rely on spices and herbs instead of fats and salt," Alison replied, educating Roslyn.

Griffin watched as Roslyn immediately turned and walked back toward the restaurant. He chuckled in amusement at her reaction.

"Where are you going?" he heard Alison call after her, surprised at the sudden departure.

"I'm getting another one," Roslyn answered, her voice getting faint as she strode back to the restaurant.

Griffin watched as Alison broke out into a jog to catch up to Roslyn. He felt an odd mix of emotions watching the two of them. Happiness battled sorrow, and Griffin reflected on Taylor's warnings about their moms. He loved seeing Alison happy and relaxed, but there was that part of him that wanted his parents to be together.

The clock tower read five minutes after five. Outside the bookstore rested the easel that had previously occupied the entry, and people trickled into the store from the cold air. It wasn't a tremendous amount of people, but the small interior made it seem that way.

A dozen people held a copy of Silence by Miles Thomas, and they gathered in the rear section of the bookstore where Miles was going to speak. Griffin and Taylor stood in the back of the crowd, but only Griffin had a copy of Silence. Alison and Roslyn joined them after a few minutes, and they exchanged quiet smiles with the teens.

With Orion next to him, Miles held a copy of Silence and walked over to a stool placed in front of the small crowd. Miles kissed Orion on the top of his head, and the clockwork plush doll Roslyn had bought for him earlier was absent.

"I'll see you after, kiddo," Miles told Orion and nudged him toward his mother.

Orion nodded and walked over to join his mom and Alison. Roslyn bent forward and hugged Orion, leaving her arm around him as she stood upright. Alison gave him a soft smile that made him grin back at her.

"Where's your clockwork doll?" Roslyn asked him, a hint of annoyance in her voice.

"I lost it," Orion admitted sadly. "Daddy said it's okay."

Roslyn pursed her lips and looked over toward Miles. It had been an expensive doll. Of course, Miles told him it was okay; he didn't spend the money on it. Roslyn wasn't sure if it had been deliberate or not, but it still ticked her off. Alison shot Roslyn a sympathetic look, feeling bad for her. "Sure. Things get lost," Roslyn replied tightly, clearly not happy.

Miles sat on his stool and faced the gathered crowd, a showman's smile on his face. "Thank you for joining me tonight. You make me feel like a rock star or something."

The crowd rewarded Miles with laughter in response to his charm. A few wore star-struck expressions on their faces, and Miles ate it up.

"Every day, we have a dozen media platforms clambering for our attention. Movies, television, websites, radio," Miles spoke, playing to the crowd. "The newest Patterson Thriller."

Roslyn knew that was a barb aimed at her, and she didn't miss the way Alison watched her for a reaction. The crowd laughed again, and Roslyn closed her eyes briefly and tried to regain control of her frayed temper. Miles had never respected what she did for a living, and it showed. She grew angry at herself for letting him get to her, and she couldn't tamp down the rising feeling of embarrassment, even though there wasn't anything to be ashamed of for being an editor. Maybe it was that Alison witnessed the slight.

"But there's something to be said for media that demands nothing. That simply waits, in silence, to be discovered." Miles stared out at the crowd expectantly, a solemn look on his face. "Maybe that's what makes media, art."

The crowd was eating it up. The people seemed to really like him and the philosophical mumbo jumbo he spouted. Roslyn didn't get why; he was a pretentious, pompous blowhard when it came to this stuff.

"And I think we all deserve more art in our lives," Miles told the audience with a reverent nod and a soft look.

Roslyn felt the bitterness well up inside her. "That rare treasure. A sensitive man," Roslyn bit out. Alison looked over at her, understanding the anger Roslyn felt. It gave Roslyn a sense of validation yet, also made her feel petty. Seeing Miles hadn't brought out the best in her.

"That's why I founded the Orion Poetry Festival," Miles went on, dishing it up for the crowd. He had them in the palm of his hands.

"What was I thinking, right?" Roslyn huffed out in irritation to no one. "He's practically perfect in every way." Roslyn shut her mouth pretty quickly once she realized that Orion could hear her. She spoke in a quiet tone, but he was right next to her.

Alison looked back to the man speaking and studied him. She could see why Roslyn had been attracted to him, but she also saw the parts of the man that irritated the woman, which had grown to resentment over time.

"That's why I started the competition for teen poets," Miles continued, promoting his good deeds. He wasn't a man that shied away from the spotlight.

"No one is perfect for everyone," Alison told Roslyn softly. It was all she could think to say to try and ease the other woman's rising temper. She imagined that if the roles were reversed, she would need someone to understand how she felt.

Roslyn looked sharply over at Alison and stared. She was surprised by Alison's comment. Shocked that Alison wasn't instantly swayed by the charm Miles doled out as so many others were. She looked back at her ex-husband, but this time, there was a smug little grin on her face. Roslyn wasn't being judged and didn't feel like she was wrong for feeling the way she felt for the first time.

"And that's why I wrote my latest collection," Miles held up a copy of Silence for emphasis. "There's discovery in silence. There's healing and understanding and growth." His voice dripped with sincerity, and he looked directly at Roslyn. "There's art."

Roslyn felt frozen in his gaze. Anger and sadness washed through her simultaneously. She was irritated with herself for momentarily falling under his spell again simply because he was a good speaker. She felt angry that he still had that effect on her; it should have worn thin after all these years, in her opinion. Roslyn didn't want to be with Miles, but she also didn't want to be driven to emotional extremes by him either. Like he was effortlessly doing to her now.

"And life without art is hardly life at all," Miles stated in a manner that made Roslyn think he was poking at her career again. "Silence is a collection of poems that are never meant to be read aloud," he explained. "With that in mind, if everyone would turn, please, to page forty-one. I'd like us all to read silently, in tandem, now."

Miles opened his book. He turned the pages to page forty-one and took a slow, deep breath, somewhat melodramatically, and began to read silently to himself. The audience that gathered exchanged a few confused looks but then followed suit. They didn't want to appear as if they didn't appreciate the message he portrayed.

Taylor stood in the back and looked around, thinking how stupid this was, and her face gave it away. Griffin, however, opened his copy of Silence with the rest of the group and began to read, his lips moving silently. Roslyn and Alison's expressions mirrored Taylor's. Orion looked puzzled, and he appeared to be in the same camp Taylor, Alison, and his mom was in but didn't want to say it because Miles was his dad.

Four people read silently, and two had turned the page, just as Miles had directed, like puppets on a string. A moment later, the other two turned their pages, their reading a little slower. Miles sat on the stool and turned his page, read the last few lines of the poem silently, then closed his book and stared out at the crowd expectantly with an earnest smile on his face.

"Wasn't that incredible?" Miles asked the audience. There was a light smattering of applause from those who had finished reading. They hadn't expected to go to a reading and read themselves; they had been prepared to hear the author read his work in his voice, but whatever. Artists were a different breed.

Roslyn and Alison exchanged sidelong glances and grinned. Those who had still been reading finished and joined in the polite applause. No one in their group had applauded other than Griffin.

Miles nodded at the applause. "Thank you. Thank you all."

Chapter Eight

Outside the brightly lit bookstore, the world had turned dark, and the temperature had dropped further. The crowd that gathered to join the reading by Miles Thomas, which had technically never happened, dispersed. A few remained to speak to the author himself in hopes that it would be speaking in silence.

Griffin approached Miles. "Thank you, Mr. Thomas. It was a great... reading." Griffin had stuttered on the last part, not sure what to call the performance.

Griffin felt a touch nervous but took his now autographed copy of Silence back from Miles, who sat on the stool holding a gold Sharpie. Orion stood next to his father and grinned at Griffin. Alison was behind Griffin with her arm around him for moral support. A fact that he appreciated given his nerves; he could always count on his mom.

"It's good to see you back, Griffin," Miles responded politely. Not friendly, but nor was he abrupt or rude.

"I wouldn't miss it!" Griffin stated enthusiastically. He loved Miles' work.

"Thank you, Mr. Thomas," Alison interjected gently.

"Right! Thank you!" Griffin said, remembering his manners. No way would he want the man to think he wasn't polite.

Miles switched his attention to Alison curiously. "You're Griffin's mom? Ali?"

Conscious of Roslyn's feelings, Alison tried to be careful in her interactions with Roslyn's ex-husband. She found herself continually putting herself in Roslyn's shoes, sure that she would be in a similar situation soon. "Alison," she corrected the man. "Yes."

"Orion told me all about your pancakes," Miles smiled. It was an attempt to make conversation with the woman his son had talked about during their afternoon together.

"They were amazing!" Orion beamed at Alison, pleased his dad remembered.

"I wasn't sure if he meant breakfast or berets," Miles joked with a nod at Griffin's hat.

Griffin and Orion laughed, but Alison and Miles simply stared at each other. Miles was trying to figure out the exact situation, and Alison didn't like that. It irritated her that she couldn't tell if Miles was poking fun at Griffin either. She was guarded and felt oddly protective of Roslyn and her feelings, as well as Orion. Not to mention her son, who she felt Miles singled out with that comment.

"Breakfast. Yes." Alison nodded, keeping her tone even. She didn't want Griffin or Orion to catch on to her growing ire.

Miles looked away from her, his attempt to play it off as unimportant. He drew Orion close and looked back up at Alison. "Well, any friend of Roslyn's is a friend of mine," he stated grandly without a single look at the woman he had married and brought a son into the world with during their time together.

Across the bookstore in the section that held filmmaking books, Roslyn half-hid behind a bookcase and watched Alison and Miles interact. She was jealous and wasn't sure she should be or even had a right to feel that way. Taylor completely ignored them and focused her attention on the books.

"Should I go rescue your mom?" Roslyn asked quietly. She wondered if she was overstepping her boundaries. She silently cursed Miles for bringing out this sudden insecurity that welled up inside.

Taylor glanced behind them and saw her mom cross her arms as she spoke to Orion's father about how interesting Leavenworth was. Taylor knew how guarded her mom was, she saw the defensive body positioning, but she appeared to be holding her own with the man. In her opinion, Miles was posturing, though he had insane levels of confidence. He was handsome and talented, she supposed. She could understand why Roslyn had been attracted to him once.

Her brother and Orion stood off to one side, and Griffin showed Orion his autographed magazine that Taylor had gotten signed earlier by Dax. From what she saw, Orion thought it was fantastic. Taylor smiled. It was nice that something so easy had made her brother so incredibly happy.

"Nope. She's good. When she's nervous, she plays

with her hair," Taylor informed Roslyn, knowing her mother well. She'd been playing with her hair often lately, and most of the time, it was after haven spoken to Jac.

She turned back, browsing the books while Roslyn studied Alison and Miles, trying to read their body language now that she knew that tidbit Taylor had handed out. Teens were a fount of information when they wanted to be.

Taylor pulled out a square, oversized book with a black and white photo of Jennifer DiMarco looking pensive on the cover. It was labeled film, and the title was Storyteller, A Day in the Life of Filmmaker, Poet, Novelist, and Playwright Jennifer DiMarco.

"Oh!" Taylor exclaimed quietly. She held it reverently in her hands. She hadn't even known that her favorite filmmaker had a book out. This find made the entire night worth the time here. She flipped through the pages carefully and studied the photos of Jennifer DiMarco on set with actors. Interspersed with the pictures were quotes about storytelling.

A particular photo caught Taylor's eye. It showed Jennifer at her desk with a laptop and a painting of her wife on the wall. The quote next to her picture read: *We can't be interesting storytellers until we're interesting people. And no one is interesting in isolation. By allowing other people into our lives, we begin to experience the world in a communal way. We share our eyes, our minds, our hearts. We become part of the world. We become interesting.*

The quote struck Taylor so much she repeated it out loud. "By allowing other people into our lives, we begin to experience the world in a communal way. We share our eyes, our minds, our hearts. We become part of the world. We become... interesting."

Taylor closed the book and turned it over to see the price. She didn't notice Roslyn watching her with interest written across her face.

"What is it, Taylor?" Roslyn asked, carefully noting the book title.

Taylor bared her teeth with a small growl of displeasure. The price of the book was astronomically high. *Yikes, that's expensive!* she thought.

"Nothing," Taylor answered Roslyn evasively. She carefully placed the book back on the shelf and made sure it was nice and straight. Taylor desperately wanted the book, but she couldn't justify a coffee table book for forty dollars. Taylor was a starving artist herself.

"Taylor! Come meet my dad!" Orion called to her excitedly.

"Yay," Taylor muttered under her breath, far less excited about the prospect. "Coming, Orion."

Roslyn smiled, having heard everything. She watched Taylor pretend to be enthusiastic for a moment, then glanced at the film book she put back on the shelf, and once more, back at Taylor. She pursed her lips thoughtfully then looked at the book again.

The kids were all asleep in the back of the car as they drove down the dark rural road toward their temporary home of the cottage. Alison sat in the passenger seat, turned, and looked back at them with a smile. She loved seeing them like this, tired from a busy day, yet, small smiles graced their peaceful faces, even in sleep.

"I don't think they ever outgrow sleeping in the car," Alison remarked fondly.

Roslyn was lost in thought and wondered if she could have handled today better than she had? What could she have done differently? "Mm-hm," Roslyn answered distractedly. Her thoughts were scattered, and she picked herself apart mentally.

Alison knew Roslyn was struggling with something and didn't really hear what she'd said. "And those alligator sausages were the best."

Roslyn nodded a little. "Absolutely," she drawled in agreement, not giving Alison the attention that she deserved.

Alison smiled and looked forward at the road. Roslyn drove for a while, and then suddenly it dawned on her what Alison had actually said. She blinked a few times, trying to make sense of it.

"Wait. What?" Roslyn glanced at Alison in confusion. She had to ask.

All Alison could do was laugh in response. Roslyn's facial expression had been priceless and worth the effort. They rode the rest of the way back in comfortable silence. Both women were more relaxed with each other and their company.

Only the kitchen light was on in the cottage. The kids were asleep up in the dimly lit loft, and all was quiet on that front, thankfully. Griffin had left his copy of Silence on the coffee table in the living room. It was propped up a bit on some magazines as if it were on display, like a centerpiece demanding attention.

Lying on the couch in her pajamas, Roslyn started at the book like it might spring to life and bite her. After a moment, she jumped up, snatched the book off the table, and rushed into the kitchen. She tossed the volume on the counter and crossed her arms, continuing to stare at it in quiet condemnation.

"Too silent for you?" Alison joked lightly.

Roslyn jerked her head up. She'd gotten so lost in her thoughts. She hadn't even noticed that Alison was in the kitchen, standing at the stove, the kettle on and heating. She glanced at the single mug and box of vegan mushroom brew on the counter and resisted making an icky face. She walked over and looked closer at the package while Alison took another mug down.

"Much. I like a little noise," Roslyn admitted sheepishly. She set the box back down on the counter.

"Big city book editor," Alison quipped. She hoped it got a little smile out of Roslyn.

Roslyn smiled the expected smile at the friendly teasing banter and watched Alison. "You couldn't sleep?" she wondered.

Alison looked down at the kettle, then over at the two mugs and box of mushroom brew. "I think I'm getting nervous for Griffin. The preliminaries are tomorrow." Alison looked up and met Roslyn's eyes. "Do you ever do that? Get nervous for Orion?" She reached up and tucked her hair behind her ears.

Roslyn nodded emphatically. "Nervous for him. Sad for him. Mad for both of us." Her expression changed to a thoughtful one. The anxious gesture had caught her eye, and she remembered Taylor's words about Alison being nervous when she played with her hair. "I think we're wired that way. As mothers."

Alison looked back down at the kettle as if she knew it was the exact temperature that she needed it to be and took it off the heat. "I... didn't carry Griffin and Taylor." Alison poured the hot water into the mugs carefully and hoped Roslyn didn't notice the way a tremble went through her with the confession. "But I love them with everything I am."

Even though it didn't smell appetizing, Roslyn accepted the mug of steaming brew that Alison held out to her. "Having a surrogate doesn't mean you're not their mom." Roslyn took a tentative sip of the drink and fought back a wince at the taste.

Alison drank some of her tea and thought about what Roslyn said. She wondered whether or not she should take a chance and share more with the woman she had begun to think of as a friend. She didn't get the opportunity to open up often, and she felt comfortable enough around this woman to consider it an option.

Roslyn looked down into her mug with a tiny frown. "What is this?"

"Mushroom tea. Do you like it?" Alison asked, taking another drink. It was an acquired taste, she supposed.

An apologetic look crossed Roslyn's face. "Not at all."

Alison laughed, which prompted Roslyn to laugh as well. It was a welcome relief for the women who didn't laugh as often as they should have. Roslyn stuck her tongue out, making a goofy face, and handed the mug back to Alison.

Chapter Nine

Day 3

At 5:00 PM, the town clock chimed five times, the bell echoing through the cold winter air. Across the long yard toward the gazebo, a crowd had gathered. They milled around, waiting for the competition to begin. A cluster of teens was in the front, the contestants for the competition. They chattered amongst themselves, eager for the festivities to start so they each had a chance to showcase their work.

Five judges sat together in folding chairs off to the side. Each wore paper pinned to their jackets that read 'Judge, Orion Poetry Festival Teen Poet Competition.' They held clipboards to take notes on and were bundled up to keep warm. They looked far more imposing than they were.

The poets had badges that read 'Teen Poet' with a number below that depicted the order in which they'd appear on the stage, selected at random. Several competitors stood around with their parents while others that were friends hovered in a group with each other, talking and laughing. One spot had a large family gathered in support of the teen competing. One poet sat alone in the grass, a number pinned to his coat.

A square paper with the number fourteen and Orion Poetry Festival Teen Poet Competition was pinned to Griffin's black winter jacket. He smoothed the number down for the millionth time and fidgeted nervously, his breathing slightly erratic. Alison and Taylor took up posts on either side of him to help keep him calm, and they both hoped he wouldn't get too lost in his head.

Roslyn moved to stand next to Alison and exchanged a knowing glance with her. She knew Alison was nervous for her son. Heck, she was too. Orion shifted and went to stand next to Griffin. He took his hand and held it, lending his support. He could understand how Griffin would feel nervous standing in front of everyone and sharing something personal. His dad said all poetry was personal.

Griffin looked down at Orion with a grateful smile on his face. Orion was certainly a special kid, and Griffin counted himself lucky to have gotten to meet him. Taylor smiled at the scene as well, having seen the move. It was sweet and considerate of Orion to help Griffin in that manner. He was an exceptionally thoughtful kid.

Miles entered the gazebo and walked up to the rail to begin his speech to the gathered poets and audience. He held a microphone in his left hand and the roster of competitors in his right. It was virtually the same thing every year. He didn't vary it much.

"Welcome, everyone, to the Orion Poetry Festival Teen Poet Competition," Miles said into the microphone, addressing the crowd. His voice boomed through the speakers until someone adjusted the volume.

Everyone applauded, eager for the event to begin and to hear the words of the talented kids that decided to compete. A lot of whom were the same kids that entered the past few years. It was rewarding to see them grow as artists and people.

Alison kept searching the crowd, looking for and hoping to spot Jac. She had promised that she would be here for Griffin, and if Jac let him down again, Alison wasn't sure what she would do. She hated seeing that disappointed and hurt look come across his handsome young face. It was even worse that it was put there by his mother.

Roslyn wasn't sure who Alison was looking for, but she had a sneaking suspicion and then looked around herself. It wasn't like she had a description to go from for Jack, so Roslyn had no idea why she looked, but it made her feel helpful even though she wasn't.

In a hushed voice, Alison mumbled, "Come on." She fruitlessly searched and continued to come up empty-handed—another let-down in a long list of them. The hurt never ended with Jac, and she was tired of feeling like an emotional punching bag for the woman.

"Let's have a round of applause for the City of Leavenworth for welcoming us," Miles encouraged the audience, and they responded with applause on cue. "And a round of applause for every young poet who will take the mic today. I know I wasn't as brave as they are when I was a teen."

The judges applauded politely, and a mix of parents and contestants joined in, even a few poets. Griffin looked all-around at the people and searched continually, not finding what he wanted to see. Or, more accurately, who he wished to see. Griffin fought back a crushing wave of disappointment and tried to hold on to hope that his mom would show up for him. Taylor watched Griffin and knew who he looked for a midst the crowd.

"Have you seen Jac?" he asked her finally. Maybe Taylor had spotted her; she was observant. She had that artist's eye that caught things others didn't.

Taylor frowned and glanced over at her mom in worry. She was afraid that Jac's not showing up would put Griffin into a tailspin. Alison shook her head no toward Taylor and continued to search the same way Griffin was. Taylor sighed unhappily.

"I'm gonna kill—" Alison began but was interrupted by Miles with the microphone.

"First to perform today is our reigning champion, Dax Linn," Miles announced with pride. He walked toward the approaching poet and handed off the microphone with a smile and a nod at the young poet.

Dax was garbed out in his combat boots with silver chains wrapped around the ankles and the leather jacket with the number one pinned to it. Dax took a moment to straighten his jacket. He beamed his confident, rock star smile to the crowd as he took to the stage, grabbed the microphone, and made his way to the rail. He walked with a swagger and displayed not a single ounce of nervousness.

Dax stood there and took in the crowd with an ease Griffin wished he had. In slow motion, Dax brought the microphone to his face. He hammed it up for the group and began another epic performance.

Griffin looked a little green around the gills. "I think I'm gonna throw up," he mumbled. Anxiety and nerves plagued him even harder now that Dax was on stage. He idolized the poet.

Still moving as if he were in slow motion, Dax ran a hand through his hair, and Taylor ogled him with an appreciative look. Dax moved the microphone close to his mouth and ran his tongue over his lips, purposely drawing the eye to his mouth.

"Toxic," Dax said. He paused for dramatic effect. Dax stared straight toward the audience as he performed. There was no journal or script in his hands, as Griffin had mentioned before. Dax spoke from memory with certainty and rapid-fire precision.

"You're throwing it at me and so it sticks.
Screaming fake news and fake science
and I'm trusting no one
but the man in the mirror,
in the mud puddle,
in the reflection of my rearview
as I tear down I-5 like it was built just for me."

Dax's performance was rock solid, and it was apparent that he was talented at the slam poetry style he spoke. It was no wonder that he was the reigning champion. He had the audience in the palm of his hand, and he knew it. Dax owned the moment.

"And you must be right
cuz you sure believe it.
And you must know me
cuz you know everything.
And there ain't never been
a man so sure as you.
There ain't never been
a judge so high.
There has never been,

in the history of time,
a father so absolutely certain
that his son is rotten to the core."

Dax stood there for a moment holding the microphone. The judges were paying rapt attention to the poet, and the crowd was silent, captivated by the passionate prose and the young man that delivered it. Then Dax barreled into the final stanza, focused and intense, his eyes piercing.

"A poet!
He screams it like he could have
screamed a dozen other slurs.
A poet!
Boy… you could have been anything.
A mechanic. A welder. A short-order cook.
Not a doctor, sure;
You ain't smart enough for that.
But a poet?
Why not just kill me?
He says it twice.
Why not just kill me?"

Dax held the silence for a moment and then spoke in a careful, meticulous voice. He lowered his volume, and softened his tone, and delivered the final punch to the gut that you came to expect with Dax's poetry.

"Because I'm a poet, Daddy.
Not a killer.
I'm sorry
you don't know
the difference."

Dax lowered the microphone and exited toward Miles as applause erupted from the audience. Dax handed the microphone off to Miles and left the stage to wild cheers. Sure, he walked with a swagger, but his performance, his words, his delivery, had earned him the right. Miles retook his place center stage.

"Thank you, Dax." Miles bowed his head and looked at his list of names, giving the audience a moment to calm down. "Contestant Two, Jenny Faraway. Please take the stage."

Jenny stepped up with a piece of paper that had her poem written on it. Her hand shook as she took the microphone from Miles and found the spot she wanted to stand on to read her poetry. She wasn't as confident as Dax but not as nervous as Griffin.

"Goodbye, Kitty," she said. She paused, then lifted her paper to read from it. Her voice trembled with nerves, but she continued. She'd come too far to let some stage fright get the best of her. She also felt that after Dax's performance, she needed to step it up.

"Soft kitty, warm kitty,
hairless ball of blur.
You are the first thing I remember.
You were the scariest thing I knew."

Griffin let go of Orion's hand and ruffled his hair as a big brother would do to a younger one. With a scowl, Orion smoothed it back down. Anxiety had a good grip on Griffin, and he started to feel panicky. He looked at his sister with a desperate plea on his face.

"Through the house you hunted.
You stalked much faster than I ever
learned to crawl."

Chapter Ten

Taylor glanced over at Griffin, feeling the weight of his stare, and she saw the panic creeping in. It was time to act, and she knew it without a doubt. Her worry for her brother crept in and leveled up as he began to open his mouth.

"Taylor," Griffin started to say. His eyes were wide as saucers, and his pupils dilated.

"Let's walk," Taylor suggested and grabbed his arm and led him away. She pulled him further from the crowd, knowing he needed space to calm down.

Orion moved and stood with his mom and Alison, who watched Taylor lead Griffin away. Orion saw the worried look on her face, and his mom shook her head sympathetically. He knew Griffin had been nervous, but he hadn't known it was that bad. Griffin was really pale and kinda shaky. He glanced back at Alison and his mom to gauge their reactions.

"He's number fourteen. There's time," Roslyn told Alison gently, doing her best to reassure her. Alison had visibly started when she realized how close Griffin was to a panic attack. Taylor seemed to know what Griffin needed, so Roslyn had put her hand on Alison's arm, hoping to offer the same soothing touch that Taylor did for her brother.

"Why such vitriol?" Jenny read her poem.
"Why such disdain?
Kitty.
What did I ever do to you?
I was only two.
I was only two."

Taylor and Griffin walked along the edge of the crowd toward the back of the park. They didn't wander too far away, but enough to give Griffin some breathing room so he could try to beat the panic down on his own without extreme measures. Taylor knew he'd get it under control enough to read his poem, but she wanted him to feel good about it.

The next reader was on the stage now. A kid named Ned Miller. He was a smaller kid but packed a big punch vocally. Taylor remembered him from last year and had been impressed by him.

"Stop!" Ned shouted into the microphone emphatically. His voice carried the nuances needed to grab the audience's attention.

"I'm shouting at the top of my lungs;
Stop!
But the world keeps spinning.
The world
keeps
spinning.
How can it spin
when Matthew is gone?

How can it spin
when the world knows
and did nothing?"

Griffin stopped in his tracks; the anxiety attack had hit him hard. *I can't do this!* he screamed in his head. Griffin even went as far as throwing down his portfolio and the magazine. He wanted to call it quits, and it made him so angry with himself that it pushed him over the delicate edge he'd balanced on mentally.

Taylor caught his arms as he swung them and tried to soothe him with touch. Something familiar to him and something that made him feel safe and loved. Only it wasn't working this time, and Griffin's agitation remained the same.

"I can't do this. I can't do it, Taylor!" Griffin cried near tears. Anger washed up the back of his throat at his display. There were too many emotional situations that bumped around inside his head, and he couldn't get a grasp on them with the nerves that the competition brought out. *How did these other kids do it?* he wondered.

The next contestant was on the stage now, a poet named Kris Weston, who began reading their poem in a soft and silky voice with clear enunciation and an engaging smile.

"I lifted him up. I held him to the sky.
I told him the truth:
Turtles can't fly!
But he didn't want to listen. He just flew.
He was a butterfly in turtle's clothing.
And butterflies
never listen."

Taylor scooped up the portfolio and magazine and grabbed the pen that had fallen loose. No way could she leave them there; Griffin would freak out if he didn't have them. "You're not giving up," Taylor demanded of her brother. Uplifting tough love might be what was needed this time around. She'd do whatever it took.

The next competitor had taken the stage by now, and another voice filled the air, this one named Lily Sustina. Her voice was melodic, and her body swayed as she talked. Taylor only glanced her way, though. Her focus remained on her brother.

"And on stage I moved like the willow tree
like the cypress, like the alder
in the springtime when everything
is new and bending, bowing down
to winds as strong as the elements.
And I knew in that moment:
Dance was not for me."

Taylor pressed Griffin's stuff back into his arms. "I won't let you walk away," she promised her brother in a firm tone. "You deserve this. Griffin. You deserve this," she assured him as the next artist took to the stage. Brenna Davis, Taylor heard in the background. She remembered this one too. She wasn't one of Taylor's favorites which made it easier to tune her out.

"I run. Faster than mayo in summer.
Slower than a hummingbird surely.
I'm looking everywhere.
Almost everywhere.

But not the gross places.
I'm like a pony who's lost
her favorite balloon."

ust like that, Brenna finished, and Todd Sheridan took the stage. All names familiar to the teens for the past six years they'd been attending the festival. Taylor didn't dare give them the attention they deserved because, to be honest, Griffin was more important than all of them. She continued to walk Griffin along, skirting the crowd and held on to his arm with her free hand.

"I sank.
Down.
Down.
Down.
Down.
The ocean was blue on top
but black underneath
like an ombre hairstyle
gone terribly wrong.
I was a creature.
I was a sea flapflap.
But without
the flapflap.
And way
too much sea."

iles called Robert Jackson up next, and Griffin continued to pace with Taylor placating him. She didn't know how to get through to Griffin at the moment, and it worried her more than she wanted to admit. She just wished that Jac would show up so Griffin could see that he mattered to more than just her and Alison. He needed her love, and it had been in short supply lately.

"Embrace what's hard," Robert's voice rang out as if he were talking to Griffin.

"Show the world
you can take it.
Decide.
Today.
To be kind."

Griffin paused his pacing. Something in those words spoke to him. He searched the crowd again, hope filling his heart that he would see the familiar face he longed to see. Taylor bit her lip, her heart breaking at the pain written on her brother's face when he didn't spot Jac.

Now Alanis Yolan was on stage reading her work after Miles handed off the microphone. It felt like they were zipping along faster than usual and Taylor worried she wouldn't be able to get Griffin to a place he needed to be in mentally for him to take the stage.

"They're dying," Alanis stated.

"You say it like you're
mentioning the weather.
You say it like you're
commenting on the news.
Casual, callus, and cold."

Taylor had lost count on what number of contestants they were on, and she knew Griffin was fourteen. She tried to listen to the number of the next reader, Markus Stripesen, as Miles called him to the stage. She must have missed it because Markus dove right into his poem without pause.

"Do I even have the energy to be mad anymore?
Do I even have the energy to roll my eyes
and hold my head in my hands?
Do I even have the energy to say it?!" Markus
cried out with emotion.

Taylor continued to do her best to calm Griffin. He finally nodded, whether it was at the words he heard someone speak or something he'd told himself she didn't know, and Griffin looked up over Taylor's shoulder toward the crowd he'd been trying to escape. His eyes briefly lit, and she knew that meant he thought he spotted Jac. Her own heart caught in her throat, afraid to hope but not wanting to dismiss it in case Jac came through.

"Contestant twelve. Sarah Alaska," Miles called out from the stage. Sarah stepped up and began to read. Her voice was captivating and drew you into her words with the dreamy tone she used to recite her work.

"The first time I saw him was at the river.
He stood on the garden bridge
and his hair was pale as his poet's shirt
and his eyes were blind.
But more open
than anyone else
I'd ever known.
He heard me approaching
and asked my name
but when he lifted his face
I saw he already knew it.
My name was whatever
he wanted it to be." Sarah smiled, then continued.

"For the first time
I was my voice.
My laughter. My words.
I wasn't just a smile.
Just a body.
Just another girl.
For the first time
I was everything I wanted to be
when he looked my way
and saw nothing.
And when we kissed?
It was also my first time.
But it wasn't my last."

Sarah's voice was strong by the end, and the sound of applause could be heard for Sarah's performance, and Griffin still stood there, staring, his face shell-shocked. Taylor turned to look and saw, standing at the back of the crowd, a short-haired woman. It was Jac, and she was locked in a passionate kiss with the woman named Kiki they'd heard about once; at least she assumed that is who it was. From this distance, Jac looked masculine, compared to Kiki's shapely, punk, and pretty appearance. Taylor's eyes narrowed into an aggravated expression.

Out of the corner of her eye, Taylor saw Roslyn and Alison standing with Orion. Alison had been watching them and turned to see what had caught her kid's attention. Dang it, Taylor had hoped that she wouldn't see Jac. She knew how much it would hurt Alison to witness that scene.

"Where's Griffin? It's almost his—" Alison froze midsentence. "Oh no."

"What is it?" Roslyn asked, looking around. She knew what it had to have been, but it hurt to look at the anguish on Alison's face.

"Jac," Alison replied bitterly. Her heart broke all over again at the scene that she knew was being purposely done to drive the point home that it was over. Sometimes Jac was just cruel.

Still kissing Kiki, Jac had her back to Griffin when he approached. That part wasn't intentional, but Kiki knew how to kiss, and she lost herself to the sensations. She didn't care if there was an audience or not. Others were just jealous of her happiness.

"Mom?" Griffin greeted her hesitantly. He wasn't even sure if she wanted to see him.

Jac turned, surprised to hear Griffin's voice behind her. Kiki draped herself over Jac possessively. "Hey there, Grif. Told ya I'd be here." Her voice came out cockier than she intended, but she'd gone out of her way to be here since Alison demanded it and said it was essential to Griffin. It was only a silly contest, and she had things to do.

"What the hell?!" Griffin exclaimed angrily. It felt like Jac had punched him right in the heart and left him bleeding.

"Hey!" Jac admonished him for the tone and language. He needed to show respect to his elders; that's how she raised him.

"You said you needed space," Griffin accused with a pointed look at Kiki. He guessed Taylor had been right, and he hated the way it felt to know his family fell apart.

"Grif." It was all Jac said, but it was relayed with a warning in her tone to remember his manners.

"You're still married!" Griffin shouted, unable to control himself or his wildly careening emotions.

The accusation pissed Jac off, and Kiki frowned, feeding off her facial expression. It wasn't as if Kiki hadn't known, that was the whole reason for the possessive display she had put on when the kids showed up, and Jac loved that feeling of being the center of the woman's world. "Because your mother won't sign the damn papers!" Jac yelled back, her temper flared.

Griffin's mouth dropped open in shock at the admission. For some reason, he had believed that his parents were just separated and going through a rough patch, not really getting a divorce. That wasn't supposed to happen. They were going to work things out, he believed. That is until Jac crushed that thought. He saw Taylor glaring at Jac, and finally, his words came. "You're my mother, too."

The silence after that statement stretched out painfully. Applause started for the competitor who had finished, and Jac cleared her throat dramatically. "Kiki?"

"Kiki?" Griffin echoed, his voice bitter. There was no use in hiding how he felt; not after he blew up.

"These are my kids, Taylor and Griffin," Jac introduced them as if nothing had happened and this was an everyday occurrence.

"Nice to meet you, Kiki," Taylor said politely, if somewhat coldly. She remembered her manners, but her patience with her mother's antics was about to explode. It was only for Griffin's sake that she held it in.

"Do you have kids?" Griffin asked Kiki. He tried to

make his voice as polite as he could, though he knew it came out in an accusatory manner.

Jac had her arm around Kiki, and the other woman was nestled up against Jac, making it clear they were together. Just in case, Alison got any wild ideas and joined in this circus.

"Contestant fourteen. Griffin Wylie," Miles called out and summoned Griffin to the stage.

"Sure do. Bobby. Sammy. Danny. Marty and Lou. They love Jac," Kiki boasted proudly, tossing the barb in like it mattered at this point.

"Five," Griffin responded bitterly. "Wow. That's not a lot of space." He didn't care if he was rude. Jac had hurt him on one of the most important days of his young life, and mothers were supposed to be there to support you. Not make it about them.

"It's just a thing people say, Grif. They need space. It's just a thing," Jac repeated, tired of the argument. She loved him, but she loved Kiki too.

Griffin was dumbfounded and shocked, silent; Taylor stood stoically behind him. "No. It's not."

"Contestant fourteen. Griffin Wylie," Miles called again, somewhat impatiently.

Taylor put her hand on Griffin's shoulder and tried to pull him toward the stage. He needed to focus on his goal, his dream, not the desperate attempt at a sad reality show that Jac was putting on.

"Words matter," Griffin declared hotly. He turned and left them standing there. He was so far out of control that he felt hopeless.

Taylor began to follow him but then paused and turned to Jac when Griffin started sprinting through the crowd toward the stage. "You're unbelievable," Taylor said snidely. She turned back to follow after her brother, leaving her oblivious mother Jac with the plaything she had with her.

"What?" Jac asked after Taylor's retreating form. She didn't understand her kid's reactions at all. They should be elated that she's happy.

Chapter Eleven

Orion pointed to the stage excitedly. "There's Griffin!"

"Oh, thank god," Alison sighed, still worried. Taylor walked up and joined their little group. "Is he okay?" Alison asked her daughter. Taylor's pinched face said more than her words did. Alison's heart clenched painfully.

Taylor shook her head. "Not really." No use in lying when she knew Alison would see right through it.

Griffin walked robotically up the stairs to the stage where Miles waited for him. Griffin blinked, trying to stop the tears from forming and falling. He felt shattered. This situation was not how this was supposed to happen. Miles gave him a concerned look.

"Griffin?" Miles asked softly. The distress was evident on the teen's face, and it was clear it was more than a bad case of nerves.

"I'm fine. I'm ready," Griffin answered despite being neither of these things. He was broken, disappointed, angry, and so desperately sad. It overshadowed the nervousness he'd been previously feeling.

Griffin held out his hand for the microphone, and it noticeably shook. Miles hesitated but gave it to him; to do anything else would be awkward and draw the wrong kind of attention to the teen. Griffin took it and walked toward the rail, keeping his eyes cast down. He lifted his portfolio and opened it to the page with his memorized poem. During that movement, the autographed Beat Poet Magazine fell and hit the stage with a loud thump.

Griffin shifted his feet around the crumpled magazine; he'd pick it up afterward. The fumble already made him feel stupid. A few of the other contestants in the audience smirked at the nervous behavior, and others felt bad; even not looking up, Griffin saw it. The judges all had their pens poised above their clipboards; their faces turned up to watch Griffin. He felt their stares.

Griffin lifted his tear-streaked face, his cheeks stained red with hurt and anger. He hated it. His voice was rough as he began to read; the emotion flowed unchecked from his mouth. It wasn't intentional, but it gave his words more power, just as the prose declared.

"Words. It's just words.

Repeated over and over.

Sticks and stones... and words."

Griffin's voice gained strength in the truth of the words he now recited and how mentally he applied them to his situation. It didn't dampen the amount of raw emotion emanating from him. Nothing could do that other than a raw release.

"But words have power.

The confession of the ages.

The secret of society.
Sticks and stones and words!"

Griffin had the attention of every single person watching, even the judges. They were captivated by how raw he was and how strong that rawness hit them. Roslyn, Orion, Alison, and Taylor listened raptly, not having heard Griffin speak this way before. It was beautiful and awful because it was real.

"Beyond pheromones.
Beyond commonalities.
It's the way we speak…"

Griffin became so lost in his poem and the feelings cascading through him he didn't notice anything but the paper in his hand. He didn't see Dax Linn leaning against the tree, listening and admiring how good Griffin was doing. He only saw his words, the same ones that echoed around in his head.

"…the words we choose
that build up or tear down
everything and everyone.
Push me away. We descend.
Draw me near. We ascend.
In language lies the strength
to rend or render friendship.
To rend or render love.
To rend or render family."

Griffin noticed only his words. Not Jac or Kiki listening attentively. Not Miles, being held captive by the performance. New tears streaked down his expressive face, his portfolio clutched against his chest, and his voice began to waver again as he slowly started to break down. There was no stopping it; it had a firm grip on him.

"Sticks and stones and words.

My victory is meaningless
Unless…"
Taylor watched Griffin. She knew the poem by heart as much as he did, and she saw him starting to fall apart. Her heart broke for him.

"Unless…"

"Unless I bring you—" Taylor murmured in a hushed tone, encouraging him even if he couldn't hear her.

Griffin's face was drenched in tears now, unabashed and flowing freely.

"Unless I bring you with me.
We rise or fall… together."

Griffin's throat closed on the word together, and he dropped the microphone. Air couldn't get through, and he felt like he was suffocating. The microphone landed with a thump on the crumpled magazine, and Griffin bolted. He was embarrassed and ashamed that he broke down in front of everyone and believed he ruined his last chance for the competition. Griffin couldn't get down off and away from that stage fast enough. Griffin's world crumbled under his feet as he darted away, humiliated with himself.

Miles had picked up the microphone and magazine by the time Griffin had cleared the stairs. "Contestant fifteen. Charles Saul," Miles called out with a parting glance at Griffins retreating form. His face creased with worry as his eyes tracked Griffin's trajectory.

Griffin ran toward his family; tears streamed from his eyes. Alison and Taylor took off from where they stood and ran to meet him with their arms open, Roslyn and Orion right behind them. Griffin threw himself into his mom's arms, a sobbing mess, and Orion threw himself at Griffin simultaneously and hugged him tightly. Taylor moved in quickly and put her arms around Griffin from behind, and Roslyn put her hand on Alison's back as a show of support. Each of them was overcome by powerful emotions that rocked them.

oslyn's SUV came around a bend in the road and drove slowly around the turn, then down the road that led back to the cottage. She felt like if she took it as fast as she wanted to, it would upset the strained balance Griffin and Alison teetered on precariously.

Orion sat in the middle of the back seat and gazed up at Griffin, who looked utterly exhausted and devastated. Orion was old enough to understand that Griffin thought he failed at the competition and that learning the truth about his parents was the most horrible thing he had ever faced. Orion understood that better than they thought. He remembered it happening to him like it was yesterday. He'd had some pretty awful days after that.

Orion carefully took Griffin's hand in both of his. It helped him when his mom held his hand when he was sad. Griffin looked down at their hands and then met Orion's gaze. Orion didn't say anything; he just leaned over and put his head against Griffin's shoulder. Griffin's eyes made him want to cry. There was so much stuff Orion could see going on behind them. He wished there was something more he could do to help.

Taylor smiled gently at the younger boy for being so sensitive to her brother's emotional needs. It didn't stop Taylor from worrying about Griffin. She couldn't remember a time ever in their lives that Griffin had lost control like that. It was a testament to how badly Jac had hurt him, and that made Taylor furious. Not just for Griffin, but the haunted look in Alison's eyes, for the pain that echoed through them all at having their lives put into a state of upheaval.

Taylor knew enough from watching the interplay between Alison and Jac over the past few years that it was possible to fall out of love. She disagreed with the way Jac handled it or how she disappeared from their lives unless it suited her to be in them. Taylor knew Jac loved them, but it wasn't the same love Alison offered, which was a rude awakening for Griffin. Taylor released a quiet sigh and leaned her head against the window, and closed her eyes.

Alison couldn't help being upset. She should have been more honest with Griffin about what was going on with her and Jac. He was old enough to know the basics without sharing the private details. Alison just wanted to protect him as long as she could, and maybe that hadn't been the right choice, or perhaps she should have allowed him to choose for himself. Being a parent wasn't easy, and she knew she made mistakes; it was bound to happen. Should Alison just have signed the papers, walked away from a nineteen-year relationship, and gotten on with her life? She wiped the tears from her eyes angrily. Jac didn't deserve these tears.

Roslyn drove and glanced over at Alison. Roslyn knew firsthand the pain that Alison felt. Miles had never caused Orion to meltdown the way Griffin had, and she was grateful for that. Roslyn was a bit surprised to see Alison remove the wedding ring, though. She looked back to the road, her heart hurting for her new friend and her son. It was devastating to witness.

There was nothing she could say to take the pain from either of them, which is why she remained quiet and just drove. They needed to feel their grief and come to terms with it. Everyone did. They had every right to feel the way they felt.

Taylor turned on the small lamp up in the loft that sat near Orion's bed. She thought that maybe the light would help Griffin feel not quite as sad. A moment later, Orion set down his glasses and turned the light off, settling on his bed. "Too much light stops the development of melatonin required for healthy sleep," Orion informed her.

Taylor shot an amused glance at Orion. She couldn't help it and sat on her bed; Taylor was tired, but the kid amused her and had wormed his way into her heart. She had a way with kids naturally but had never grown attached this quickly before. There was every chance this one could wrap her around his finger if he put his mind to it. "Okay, Orion. We just have different habits in our family."

Griffin lay in his bed, and his eyes opened as he obsessed over the whole horrible evening. He replayed it over and over in his head. An endless movie reel that felt like a nightmare that wouldn't stop. He'd botched everything; responses to Jac and the competition. Not to mention breaking down like a lunatic with a group of peers and judges watching.

"We're surprisingly alike," Orion commented, getting himself situated in the large bed. He wanted to make them feel better, and he had been working on a way to do so the whole way back.

Taylor swung her legs under the blankets. She looked between Orion and Griffin, distracted with worry over her brother, but she wanted to be nice to the kind little boy. Griffin hadn't moved an inch, Taylor noticed. She knew he was awake, though, and could hear Orion. "Oh yeah?"

Orion took a moment to think before he answered. He mulled it over whether or not he would share this fact about his mom. Orion had read in the magazine that Taylor and Griffin had two moms, and that was what finally tipped the scales to make him decide to tell his truth. Or his reality as he understood it. He understood a lot more than people gave him credit for knowing.

"My mom is gay," Orion finally said, just tossing the declaration out there.

Taylor sat up in bed and looked over toward Orion. She didn't know if he could see her face or not, but he had her complete attention. It also started to make a little plan form in her mind. Even if love wasn't in the cards for either Alison or Roslyn, they might be what each other needed to get them through their hurt. Plus, she'd noticed the way Roslyn looked at Alison. It was hard to miss.

"That's why my parents are divorced," Orion explained. He hoped that Griffin was listening. "She used to cry all the time. Sometimes Daddy would cry too." Orion's tone was utterly serious. "They don't cry anymore." While that was true, his mom still got upset by his dad. Orion didn't know enough about why to speak about that. He just knew she got tensed up and pinched looking when he talked about his dad.

Griffin found himself pulled out of his misery and listened to the young boy. He hadn't known Roslyn was gay, nor that her divorce had been recent. Not that it made a difference in how Griffin saw her, but it helped him understand Orion a bit more. Knowing that he'd been old enough to understand the divorce and the reasons why helped Griffin feel less alone, and it warmed his heart that Orion's reaching out was his way of trying to help Griffin cope.

Taylor, Orion, and Griffin remained still, quiet, and contemplative until they all fell asleep. Orion's message had landed with his desired effect, and maybe even more than he'd hoped. They had a lot to think about, and divorce affected them all, not just Griffin, though his hurt was more pronounced.

In the bedroom Alison was occupying, her door was half-opened. A small lamp shone from inside the room and cast a shadow on the hallway. Roslyn approached with a soft step and knocked gently on the frame. She didn't want Alison to feel left out and alone to deal with the heartache or that she couldn't express her emotions.

"Alison?" Roslyn called out quietly and poked her head into the room.

It appeared that Alison was asleep. Roslyn couldn't be sure, though. Her back was to the door, and her breathing was a steady rhythm. It could be faked; Roslyn had done that herself a time or two. She watched for a moment and glanced around the room. Roslyn also noticed that Alison's wedding ring now lay on the bedside table near the lamp. Next to that was a manila envelope, filled with the divorce paperwork Roslyn assumed, and a pen lying on top. The ring and the pen on the envelope told Roslyn all she needed to know.

Roslyn lingered in the doorway for a moment and hoped that Alison would roll over and invite her in. Her heart broke for the pain that she knew Alison was going through and all that she had witnessed earlier tonight. She wished Alison would reach out and ask for help or just try to talk things out. Not seeing Alison respond, Roslyn turned and went quietly back down the hallway.

Alison lay on her side and faced the wall. Hot tears slid down her face and soaked into the pillow. Her eyes were open, and she'd heard Roslyn, but she wanted to be alone. She figured she'd be that way for a while. Shame, anger, heartbreak, love, it all washed through her. She'd signed the papers, and it felt like she ripped her heart out and sliced it open. Jac had hurt her too many times now.

Alison wasn't stupid enough to think Jac was the only one to blame, but today's experience took it to another level. Seeing the way she had flung her new lover in Griffin's face stung more than she cared to admit, and that was all it took to push the decision-making process over the edge. The hurt look on Griffin's face helped her to understand that she wanted nothing to do with Jac anymore. It was over. The thought both caused anguish and a sense of freedom.

Chapter Twelve

Day 4

The mountains that surrounded Leavenworth were all capped in snowy peaks. The view was dramatic, stunning, and one would be hard-pressed not to stop and gape at the natural beauty. Tree branches were heavy with the wintery white substance, and it created a peaceful backdrop and inspired thoughts of a warm fire and a cup of cocoa. It was a wonderland.

Griffin stood at the riverside and exhaled a cloud of warm breath. The air was icy, and the water was beyond frigid. But it was serene, and he needed that more than anything. It was a calm and soothing scene that directly contrasted the raging storm of emotions that bounced around inside him. He wiped at his eyes, trying not to cry. He shifted his stance, feeling restless, and tried to regain control of his emotions. Upset was an understatement of epic proportions. The moment in front of the river stretched out as he stood there, motionless, despite his need to move.

Griffin reached up and took off his beret in a symbolic gesture of giving up. Nothing seemed worth it anymore. His thoughts turned dark and brooding. He'd blown his last chance of winning the festival and went down in a blaze of embarrassment. His parents were never getting back together, and he felt utterly powerless, disappointed, sad, and angry.

His breathing grew heavier, and the conflicted emotions inside were mirrored on his face, and it was evident. He warred with feeling guilty, sorrowful, and even angry, which wasn't normal for him and surprised him. The situation was incredibly painful for Griffin, every last bit of it. His family was everything to him. Like Alison, Griffin didn't do angry well, or more truthfully, at all. It wasn't a good feeling to harbor inside.

Roslyn walked outside on the back deck of the cottage, the door gently closing behind her. She walked across the deck and down the stairs, talking on her cell phone away from where others could hear her conversation. Some things Orion didn't need to overhear, and she didn't want to burden Alison with more things to worry about; she had enough going on.

"Miles, if the PA system is down, you need to get it fixed. Who's going to come out on a Saturday? Just call Orion and tell him you'll see him tomorrow," Roslyn suggested. She paused at the bottom of the stairs and took in the views.

Roslyn felt the frustration build because Miles was acting incredibly considerate, which she wasn't used to with him. He'd called to tell her he'd be an hour late picking up Orion from Leavenworth. Before, he'd just be late and made her wait with no explanation or warning that he wasn't going to be on time.

"Fine. Okay, I'll have Orion in town at noon instead of ten. Thanks for letting me—" Roslyn was interrupted by a loud scream of frustration coming from Griffin that echoed a bit. She looked up in concern, already lowering the phone from her face as she spoke. "I gotta go."

Roslyn hung up the phone and quickly and carefully navigated her way in the direction she'd heard the shout, which was down toward the river. Worried he'd fallen and hurt himself, she wanted to run but knew that wouldn't be a good idea.

Roslyn hustled as best as she could to the embankment that overlooked the river and paused. She sharply inhaled as she took in the scene, the cold air burning her lungs as she gulped in air. Griffin was the first sight, and she was thankful he stood there unharmed; then, she noticed the raspberry beret as it floated down the river on the current. That wasn't good.

Griffin stood on the riverbank, upset, frustrated, and glaring at the beret as it drifted away. He'd reached his breaking point, and the noise in his head wouldn't take a break. From the corner of his eye, Griffin spotted Roslyn carefully making her way toward him, then the sound of her movement hit his ears, and he closed his eyes. Griffin wasn't sure he wanted company or a witness to another of his breakdowns.

Roslyn stepped up beside Griffin and faced the river with him. She remained silent and just stood in solidarity next to his side as a show of support. The gesture was kind, and he appreciated it. He cleared his throat a little, aware that Roslyn had heard him shout if she had come to investigate.

"Sorry," Griffin apologized. "I'm fine." He finally broke the silence and addressed the elephant in the river, so to speak. His beret was the only spot of color as it drifted. He knew she saw it.

Roslyn kept her head straight ahead and didn't look at him. She knew he was embarrassed to be caught venting. She understood the war inside him better than he thought. "No, you're not." She felt Griffin's eyes on her then. "And you don't have to be sorry."

Roslyn continued to view the cold river, and Griffin watched her, unsure how to feel about her statement. He absorbed her words and thought about it, probably more than necessary, though he appreciated her saying them. It was nice to know someone didn't believe Griffin was a complete wreck, even if he felt it about himself. Also, it felt good to hear that he wasn't wrong to feel the way he did.

"I'm pretty pissed too. Whatever happened to global warming? It's colder than hell out here!" she declared as a way to ease his tension. She hoped for a smile at a minimum so she could see the happy Griffin was still inside him, even if he got pushed out of the way for a moment.

"Roslyn!" Griffin scolded her for the foul language.

"You're right. Everything is colder than hell, right?" Roslyn joked. She had to keep trying. Griffin was a pretty fantastic teenager, and she hated to see him so down. Not only upset with himself but the things that were outside of his control.

Griffin managed a small smile and shook his head at her antics and methods of trying to cheer him up. It was apparent what she was doing. It was a kind gesture, and her company wasn't entirely unwelcomed, despite his initial misgivings at her appearance. He turned his head to look at her, feeling able to meet her gaze.

"Griffin. It's all right to be mad. It seems like your mom... Alison doesn't really do mad, huh?" Roslyn offered up as a conversation starter. She thought he might need to hear that it's okay to be mad and disappointed by a parent.

"No," Griffin admitted. They were a lot alike in that way. It wasn't something he had actively thought about before, and it took Roslyn pointing it out for him to see it. It was an interesting fact.

"Maybe mad scares her. Mad scares a lot of women. But you're not your mom," Roslyn continued to encourage him, slowly turning the conversation to him and his feelings. She went with her gut instinct and continued. "You're you. And maybe you do mad."

Griffin listened and watched Roslyn's face for signs of false platitudes. He didn't see any, and her words felt genuine. They also resonated deep inside the hurricane that tore him up inside. Her comments sparked something, and the fuse lit, even if it began as a slow burn.

"Maybe everyone should do mad, sometimes," Roslyn stated as if to herself. She went silent a moment before she continued. Roslyn saw that she was getting through by the spark in his eyes. But it wasn't a word she spoke when she broke the silence. She shouted loud, letting it bellow from deep in her gut, just as Griffin had earlier when it scared her.

Griffin jumped a little and gave her an astonished look. He hadn't expected that at all, and she'd caught him off-guard. Roslyn smiled and nudged him with her elbow, prodding him. She let out another shout, not quite as loud as the first, and gave him an encouraging smile. It didn't take Griffin long to think about it; the need burned through him, from his toes to his head. He let out another mighty shout that came from the depths of his soul and carried all the anger and grief he felt.

Birds scattered from the trees they perched in as the sound echoed across the wintery scene. Griffin had to admit that it felt good. It was freeing to let all that toxicity out from inside where it ate at him. He wasn't used to harboring emotions like that, and he guessed they had been on a slow build since Jac had left. Seeing her with Kiki had only pushed him right over the edge. Roslyn was an intelligent woman to know that was what he'd needed. He certainly hadn't been able to figure it out while he stood there and froze.

After another few silent moments, they turned away from the river and began to walk back toward the cottage at a slower pace than when Roslyn had come down since there was no rush or something that made them worried. Roslyn tucked her cell phone back into her pocket, so she didn't drop it and break it, which she had done before when she wasn't paying attention to what she was doing.

"Were you talking to Mr. Thomas?" Griffin asked out of curiosity. He knew it wasn't his business, but he was curious about the woman, and he hoped she would answer.

"Yep," Roslyn straightforwardly confirmed without hesitation.

"Did he say something that made you mad?" Griffin wondered, feeling oddly protective of Roslyn after she helped him. It was because of her that he got through that awful moment down at the river. Griffin felt like he owed her the same.

"He never does. That's what pisses me off," Roslyn explained evasively.

Griffin paused, contemplating Roslyn's words. He didn't think that was an entirely true statement, though he was hesitant to call her on it. She'd been honest with him, and she was entitled to her privacy, especially on something as personal as her divorce. Roslyn had continued her trek back to the cottage, and Griffin hustled to catch up to her.

"Roslyn?" Griffin called out. She paused, half-turned, and waited for him. Griffin felt the need to try and soothe some of her hurt the way she'd relieved his. "Robert Frost wrote for two audiences: Academics and the rest of us. He had two layers to all his poems so they could be experienced in two totally different ways. He did it on purpose."

Roslyn listened to Griffin's explanation with a grateful expression, and it became clear that he had overheard her conversation with Alison when she'd explained her reaction to Orion's deconstruction of her favorite poem. She didn't mind, and she appreciated Griffin's effort more than she could say.

"It's one of the things that makes him such a great writer," Griffin commented, pleased to see her face soften and her eyes warm at the comment.

"Who's your favorite?" Roslyn wondered, genuinely curious to learn more about this complex young man.

"Whitman," Griffin responded immediately. "He was such a fox." Griffin grinned widely and continued walking, leaving Roslyn behind him a few steps.

Roslyn let out a loud laugh and followed after him, delighted by Griffin's whit. "More like a bear."

Alison accidentally slept in for once. She cracked an eye open and wondered why her alarm hadn't woken her. Alison sleepily sat up and scrubbed her hands over her face trying to wipe the sleep away. She looked around for her phone and found it on the nightstand. Picking it up, she pressed the home button but found the phone completely dead. That's why her alarm didn't wake her. *Crap!*

"Hey, sleepy head," Roslyn said from the doorway softly.

Alison looked up at the bedroom door, and once her eyes focused, she saw her kids, Roslyn, and Orion all dressed and wearing their winter coats. She briefly wondered how long she'd slept and then took a closer look at Griffin's face because that was more important to her. He still appeared somewhat reticent, but nothing like he was the night before, which was a massive relief for Alison. Not that she wasn't still worried, but his mental state appeared much better this morning. She wondered what had brought him out of that.

Taylor, of course, had her Super 8 hanging from her shoulder and looked picture perfect. Some things would never change. Though it didn't escape her notice that Taylor kept casting furtive glances at her brother with mild concern. Not the outright panic she'd seen on Taylor's face last night.

"Breakfast. My treat," Roslyn told her, drawing her attention from her kids.

"Golden Grill!" Orion cheered, excited, and ready

to get going.

Alison smiled up at them gratefully and nodded. She waited until they retreated from the door before she moved. She got up and began her morning routine of getting ready and then happily met the rest to have a late breakfast. Or given the late hour an early lunch. She found herself looking forward to the outing, which surprised her after the heavy emotions she'd felt about Jac last night.

Roslyn drove, which gave Alison a moment to relax and try to collect her thoughts. She looked over her shoulder at the kids in the backseat and asked Orion, "So, what's the Golden Grill?" she wondered with a smile at the look that lit the boy's face.

"It's amazing!" Orion exclaimed, bouncing in his seat a little. He didn't offer any further explanation, just beamed out an anticipatory smile.

"It's Orion's favorite," Roslyn added with a grin. Happiness washed over her at the much less tense atmosphere in the car. Last night had been almost unbearable. These smiles were heartwarming, even if Griffin's wasn't as bright as usual. It was still there.

The mystery was solved for Alison when they walked into a restaurant where they grilled the food the customer chose. A long glass-covered counter with a large selection of vegetables lay before them in a buffet of delight.

"It's an invention," Orion said gleefully, finally willing to explain the place. "You're inventing your meal!"

Orion led Alison through the process of selecting what they wanted in their bowl. He was a pro at this, after all. "You choose whatever you want. Meat, more meat," Orion chanted.

"But I'm a vegetarian," Alison protested with a smile. She selected some of her favorite vegetables from the selection. She gently placed them in her bowl as if she were proving a point.

"That's okay," Orion shrugged. "I still like you."

Alison laughed and continued to choose the vegetables she wanted. Orion was a precious and precocious child that delighted her to no end. His humor had perfect timing, and that made him even more charming for an almost eight-year-old.

"There are tons of vegetables, too. But don't pick the shrimp," Orion advised with a serious expression.

Alison hadn't intended to. "How come?" she wondered, curious as to Orion's statement.

Orion pushed his glasses up his nose. "Cuz then you can't kiss my mom," he stated in a matter-of-fact tone that only a child could deliver and not have it sound like a setup. "She's allergic."

Orion piled more meat in his bowl and was oblivious to his mom's mortified look and the hand she slapped over her face in embarrassment. Alison giggled and smiled at the precocious boy and followed him down the counter. The statement startled something deep inside Alison, and she was surprised to discover that the thought might have already been there even if she hadn't been aware of it.

"Good to know," Alison answered with another laugh. Orion was observant of things she didn't expect him to see since she hadn't overtly noticed it herself. Though, to give herself some credit, the events of the past few days had her off her game.

"Shrimp isn't a vegetable, Orion," Roslyn reminded him. It was the only thing she could think to say, and it did nothing to cover her embarrassment. At least Alison hadn't cringed at the thought. She'd only done that laugh that made Roslyn's stomach fill with butterflies.

"Right, right," Orion mumbled, more focused on the food and filling his bowl.

Everyone continued loading their choices into their bowls, with Griffin and Taylor at the rear of the line. Taylor found the comment just as amusing as Alison had, though Griffin hadn't heard a thing because he was so focused on his selections. She wondered how he'd feel about that? It was hard for him to think of Alison and Jac not being together, as demonstrated last night. She'd just have to pay closer attention to him.

When they got to the counter and handed the cook their bowls, he took them, flipped them over on a large, circular grill with ease, and managed to keep each separate. He was the grill master, and his movements were practiced and precise. He slid his spatula around each one, cooked the food to perfection, plated it, and handed it back.

Headed for a table that could seat six, the group carried their full plates and sat down to eat. Roslyn pulled a chair out for Alison so they could sit next to each other, but Orion darted in and sat down before she could offer it up. He began to wolf his food down without a second thought and no indication that he thought the chair was for anyone other than him. Alison smiled at Roslyn over Orion's head, and each of them sat on either side of Orion.

Griffin sat next to his sister, noticeably distracted. He ate but didn't really taste anything; he mostly stared off into the distance and looked pensive. Taylor ate because she was hungry, and the food smelled fabulous, but she watched her brother, knowing something was wrong. His mood was different than it was the night before. Better in some ways, and just different.

"Where's your beret?" Taylor asked between mouthfuls of food. Her eyes flicked to his hatless head and back to his face. It wasn't often that he didn't wear it. He considered it lucky.

"Hm?" Griffin responded distractedly. "I just... forgot it." Griffin kept his answer evasive because if he told them what he'd done, they all, except Roslyn, would have many more questions for him, and he wasn't ready to answer those yet.

Taylor grew more concerned, but Griffin wasn't talkative. She knew he would when he was ready, but the flip side of that was she hoped Griffin didn't bottle it up until he exploded like he did last night. Release was good, though that kind of release was mentally exhausting.

Across the table from Griffin, Orion's plate was totally empty, and he stared at Alison expectantly as she ate. "Do you like it?" Orion asked, visually gauging how much food she had left on her plate. She wasn't eating very fast, and he wondered if she didn't like it.

Amused, Alison finished chewing her food and swallowed before answering. "Absolutely." She took another big bite to prove her point and reassure him that she loved it.

"My mom doesn't cook," Orion stated, reaffirming his mother's statement from the other day.

He rather enjoyed Alison's cooking. However, Golden Grill was still his favorite. Plus, it made him happy that Alison liked it, even if she didn't have meat to go with all those vegetables.

"It can be very time-consuming," Alison defended Roslyn with a kind tone. She knew how hard it was to raise kids and manage a career, much less take care to work on a marriage.

"She burns water," Orion declared earnestly. His little face bore no signs of a joke whatsoever.

Alison didn't know how to respond to that. "Oh." It didn't seem likely, though, from the little she knew of Orion, she didn't think he was lying or poking fun at his mother.

"It's true," Roslyn interjected on Orion's behalf. It wasn't exactly a proud moment for her, but she might as well lay the cards out on the table and see if Alison was interested in her hand.

"Maybe she doesn't have the right recipes," Alison tried again. She kept throwing lines out for Roslyn to grab on to, only she kept letting herself drown. It was rather endearing.

"She knows where all the restaurants are," Orion added, trying to be helpful and missing the point Alison tried to make.

"I could write down a recipe for a stir fry for her. Just like Golden Grill," Alison offered. This time the statement was directed at Roslyn herself. It would give her a reason to stay in contact with the woman after this week was finished.

"I would love that," Roslyn said around Orion. She exchanged a somewhat intimate glance with Alison, and they both returned to eating. Maybe hope wouldn't be so bad to hold on to when it came to Alison and the feelings she brought out in her.

Orion looked from one to the other and smiled. He was doing whatever he could to help them get closer. His plan had perfectly worked because they were bonding like he had hoped they would. It was time his mom had someone like Alison in her life.

Chapter Thirteen

Holding hands with Miles, Orion turned and waved goodbye as he and his father walked away down the street to spend the day together. He wondered what his mom and Alison would do and bet it would probably be fun. Orion did have fun with them when he spent the day with them. Oh well, he'd have fun with his dad too.

Roslyn and Alison stood side by side on the street and watched the young boy walk away. Roslyn exhaled noisily. She never liked watching him walk away. Miles was a good father, but Orion would always be her baby, and watching him leave was hard; they were only kids for a while. "Guess it's the four of us," Roslyn began to say.

Taylor and Griffin were already in the process of walking away. Roslyn hadn't even finished the sentence before Taylor dragged Griffin with her. Taylor turned when she heard Roslyn and stepped backward. "Thanks for brunch, Roslyn! It was really good!" She grinned and kept walking. She'd caught on to Orion's plan, and she wholeheartedly agreed with it, even if he hadn't shared what he was up to with them. Taylor was just intuitive that way.

Roslyn looked back at Alison, who was watching the teens with an amused expression. Alison didn't look surprised in the least at their departure. "Dinner at Mozart's! Six o'clock." Alison glanced over at Roslyn in confusion. "I made reservations," Roslyn shrugged. She wanted to take them all out. It wasn't fair that Alison cooked for all of them all the time.

Alison stared at Roslyn for a moment, trying to figure out what she would say next. "Cocoa? My treat." She hadn't expected the dinner plans and was oddly pleased that Roslyn had taken the time to make them.

"Perfect. I'll pay," Roslyn agreed quickly. It meant more time spent with this incredible woman. They started down the street, with Alison leading the way to her favorite place for some hot cocoa.

"That's not what 'my treat' means," Alison argued over her shoulder. She was about two steps ahead of Roslyn.

"I want to talk to you about Griffin," Roslyn changed the subject and lengthened her stride to match Alison's step.

Taylor walked through the streets of the festively adorned Leavenworth. Lights, decorations, and holiday spirit were in full swing, and it gave her warm feelings of joy to see it all. Griffin walked beside her, still distracted and not his usual self. It was as if he didn't even notice all the best parts of the holiday season.

"You never forget your beret," Taylor brought up, feeling the urge to try again to get to the bottom of

Griffin's mood. She only wanted to help him and had his best interest at heart.

Griffin immediately walked away and crossed the street to be by himself. He didn't say anything, just left. Griffin felt sort of wrong, but he needed space to think. He knew Taylor meant well and was only trying to help. However, he didn't feel like letting someone else dig through his thoughts. They weren't even clear to him, let alone trying to explain them to someone else.

"Don't let Jac ruin this, Griffin," Taylor continued to talk, not having noticed that he no longer trailed after her. She took for granted that he wouldn't walk off on his own. "I know it's hard. But Jac, she was so critical and self-absorbed. Even when we were little, she had to be the best just because she carried us. But Ali's been with us from day one. She was always more of a mom, always focused on us first. They haven't been happy in so long."

Taylor looked over to where Griffin had been, expecting to see him listening to her, and saw he was gone. She stopped in her tracks and looked around, not spotting him. It went to show how far off-kilter his mood was; things like this didn't happen with Griffin. She checked up and down the street to no avail, thinking he might have spotted something in a window that drew his attention. "Griffin?" she called out. Not hearing a response, Taylor sighed heavily; worry and concern furrowed her brow.

Griffin looked up at the Gazebo, and his mind went into a black and white replay flashback, shot number four hundred and forty-seven of the microphone dropping on the magazine as he fled the stage in tears. He squeezed his eyes shut, embarrassed and disappointed in himself. As if those weren't bad enough, shame was present too. It wasn't something that he was used to feeling.

Griffin was very much a live-and-learn type of person. He didn't have many regrets and took things that he considered to have messed up as a stepping stone to better himself. Shame was a foreign feeling to him, and it wasn't one he particularly liked experiencing.

Another replay unwound through Griffin's mind. This time it was a reel of things he had noticed but not paid much attention to in the heat of the moment during his breakdown. *Orion's mouth opened in shock, Roslyn with a pitying look on her face, Alison gasping, and Taylor running across the ground to meet him. Kiki looked confused, and Jac looked disappointed and mad. The judges had exchanged glances and made notes, while others shook their heads in pity.*

Griffin opened his eyes and came to terms with the idea that he'd blown his chances. He looked down to the side and shook his head at himself. Griffin accepted that the responsibility for his actions was his own. After a moment, he sighed and turned to leave, but the sound of his cell phone dinging stopped him. He fished it out of his pocket, feeling forlorn.

Griffin looked down at the phone to see a text from an unknown number. It read: *Griffin, the official announcement will be tomorrow morning but Orion thought you'd want to know now.* It took a moment for the words to sink in. *The judges were very impressed by your vulnerability and the maturity of your theme.*

Griffin stared in amazement at the words on his screen, distracted only by the sound of another text coming in. The first message still rattled around inside his mind, and understanding dawned.

You're in the finals, Griffin. See you on Monday.

Griffin was shocked. More than shocked. He was almost overcome with joy and couldn't make himself move from where he stood. He looked up from his phone and began looking around, and he spotted Orion and Miles standing on the gazebo stage. Miles stood holding his cell phone in front of him, having just texted. Orion waved excitedly, and Miles gave Griffin a tip of the hat motion.

Griffin couldn't stop the smile that spread from ear to ear. He felt unbelievably grateful that Roslyn and Orion landed in his life and that Orion had the foresight to have his dad text him the good news before it became officially announced. He went to tip his beret back at Miles and realized—suddenly remembering— that he'd thrown his beret in the river! *Oh no!* Griffin panicked briefly and then bolted from the park, pulling up the Uber app on his phone. His emotions the past few days had veered drastically, and it was hard to keep up with himself.

Roslyn and Alison clinked their cups of hot cocoa together in cheers. Alison sipped slowly from her mug and looked around the busy and festive coffeehouse, the bustling people shuffling in and out and the rich smells of coffee. Alison looked back at Roslyn but couldn't read the expression on the other woman's face. Sometimes her poker face was beyond impressive.

"What are you thinking?" Alison wondered, daring to ask for a peek into Roslyn's thoughts. She *had* said she wanted to talk about Griffin, and Alison couldn't help but be concerned by that. Yet, Alison also didn't want to bring the mood down since she felt happy and relaxed. If Roslyn wanted to talk about Griffin, it was something to do with his spirit. It needed to get addressed, granted; only she wanted a few moments of peace.

Roslyn was looking off into the distance but not seeing anything. She felt a little disappointed with herself. Roslyn had that thought more than once the past few days. She looked over toward Alison after she realized that she'd been asked a question. "Hm? Oh," Roslyn smiled to herself. She took a sip from her cocoa. "This morning. I should have said: Good morning, Sleeping Beauty."

Alison flushed. "Oh, been there done that. Not into Prince Charming." She stared down into her cocoa as if it were the most fascinating thing she'd ever seen. There wasn't any reason for her to be embarrassed talking to Roslyn, yet the confession she was about to make had her not wanting to meet Roslyn's gaze. "I signed the paperwork last night."

Roslyn gave her a moment to come to terms with the words she'd just put out into the universe for the first time. She knew how hard it was to admit something that you worked so hard for was over. "I heard Taylor talking to you last night. On the way to the car."

"Yeah," Alison replied, still unable to meet her eyes. It was nice to talk to someone that had a marriage end not so happy and know that she wasn't alone in the conflicting emotions that washed through her.

"Griffin saw your ex before he performed?" Roslyn persisted. She wasn't trying to bully Alison, though it might feel that way to her. She also knew that if she pushed for answers, it would give Alison a chance to air it all and let some of the festering anger out. There was a method to her madness, and under it all, Roslyn only wanted to help Alison. Too often, strong females didn't reach out when they needed help, and Alison needed to understand that it was okay.

Alison fidgeted her fingers over her mug, unable to fight the restless feeling that crept through her veins. She looked up briefly and met Roslyn's eyes. "I think, until last night, Griffin really thought we'd get back together." She shook her head and looked down at her mug again, anger surging again. "I don't know why I didn't sign a month ago. The kids'll be heading off to college. It wasn't about them. It was just... he always seemed more sensitive than the other kids his age. And way more than Taylor." She didn't need to name Griffin specifically; Roslyn knew who she referenced.

Alison sighed profoundly and lifted her cocoa. She sat there in comfortable silence for a moment and let the background noise of the other shoppers and life going on normally soothe her while she drank the cocoa. She reviewed a few of the thoughts that were jumbled up in her head and began to sort them into the boxes where they belonged. Some needed to be sealed shut and stored away in the back recesses of her mind, never to see the light of day again.

"I can't hide the truth from him. Jac's already living with another woman," Alison finally said sadly. What hurt her the most was that Jac's actions made her feel like she wasn't enough and Alison was too easily replaced. Like their entire life together had been nothing more than a placeholder until Jac found something she thought better.

Roslyn nodded in understanding. That hadn't been the case with her and Miles, though it had with a lot of other women she knew. "A lot of men are like that. Bouncing between relationships."

Alison felt confused for a moment and then realized that it was time to tell Roslyn about Jac. It only was when Roslyn mentioned men that she realized Roslyn thought Jac was a Jack. She reached a hand out and laid it on the table between them. "Roslyn, Jac isn't—"

Roslyn interrupted whatever Alison had been about to say. "I almost forgot! Griffin's beret. Where did you get it?" Roslyn wasn't sure she was ready to hear more about Jack; it reminded her that Alison was a straight woman, and that didn't offer up much hope in the way of something more than friends with this unique woman.

"What?" Alison asked, confused at the abrupt change in subject. Of all the aspects of Griffin's past few days, his beret wasn't what she expected to be talking about with Roslyn.

"He was upset this morning," Roslyn began to explain. She talked with her hands to add emphasis to her words. "I saw him by the river. His beret was way out in the water."

"Oh my god," Alison breathed out in concern. The subject change made sense now. Griffin loved that beret and for him to throw it in the river said nothing good about how he felt and handled the emotions that tumbled through him. What would make him throw out his lucky hat?

"Did you buy it here?" Roslyn pressed, wondering if they could replace it. That would be the easiest solution, and she'd noticed a hat store in town that they could check with after they finished their cocoa.

"I'm the worst mom in the world," Alison moaned. She buried her face in her hands and felt her heart crack open again. She should have been there for her son as that was a moment that he was obviously in need, and she'd let him down by sleeping in late.

"Alison," Roslyn softened her tone and reached out to touch her. She set her hand down over Alison's that still rested on the table after she lifted her head. "I don't mom-shame. I'm not judging you. Each of us can only do our personal best. There's no competition. If we help each other, we all win." They were simple words for a situation that was anything but simple.

Alison took in Roslyn's words and considered them. With Jac, everything was a competition. If Alison found a small gift for one of the kids that she knew they would like, Jac would look for something bigger, more expensive, and get that to outshine Alison. Ultimately it benefitted the kids, which is why Alison would overlook it, but Roslyn's words resonated. It took a moment, then Alison responded. "He was thirteen. The first year he competed. I found it for him at The Hat Shop."

Roslyn finished her cocoa and smiled. "Let's go." They had some hat shopping to do, and hopefully, Alison would see that she was an extraordinary mother and nowhere near the awful one she thought she was. If they could replace Griffin's hat, maybe it would help give him a new outlook, and Alison too.

Inside The Tea Shop, amidst the fragrant leaves, Taylor fawned over containers of loose-leaf teas with literary-themed names after poets and writers. The last in the line of those teas was a Walt Whitman tea. Taylor reached for it and picked it up. She wondered if that would cheer Griffin up. Taylor studied the tea blend and turned the container over in her hands. She sniffed at it too and found the scent soothing.

"You don't look like a Whitman fan," Dax stated as he walked up to Taylor, his swagger present. He radiated confidence. Or perhaps it was arrogance.

Taylor screwed her face up in confusion. *What does that mean?* She turned to look at him. He stood close behind her, and when she turned, the canister of tea was the only thing between them. He'd invaded her space, and she couldn't decide if she liked it or not.

"Oh," Taylor said softly, resisting the urge to step back and put space between them. Despite the cockiness, she found herself intrigued by Dax. She wanted to see what would happen next.

"Buying for someone special?" Dax asked conversationally. Truthfully, he was fishing for more information on the beautiful woman.

"Yes. I mean, no. It's for my—" Taylor began to explain, slightly flustered. He was certainly lovely to look at; she just wasn't entirely sure that everything below the surface was what she wanted.

"Too focused on film to date, Fellini?" Dax cajoled, interrupting Taylor.

Taylor was unimpressed and unsurprised by that question. She figured he would have gotten around to asking sooner rather than later. *Let the sparring begin,* she thought. "Fellini? There are female filmmakers."

Dax was smooth and wickedly intelligent, with a certain charm that usually had women eating out of his hand. Writing, film, and art were his specialty; a way with females wasn't far behind those in his talents. "Sure. Bigelow, Coppola, Morano."

With the canister of tea still held between them, Taylor cocked her head to the side, not overly impressed that he named the more well-known filmmakers. "Morano? Try Marshall, Campion, Jenkins." Taylor wasn't going to pull any punches, but she found herself enjoying the conversation despite her misgivings about the man himself. There were still some red flags that had her holding back.

"Morano's a firebrand," Dax replied, at ease with the conversation. He was pleased that Taylor knew what she talked about. Some of the women he encountered weren't overflowing with intelligence.

"Palcy and Dash are firebrands," Taylor argued, standing her ground. Sure it was a matter of taste. However, some things set some filmmakers apart from others, and she wanted to be one of those.

An employee of the shop walked up and stood just beyond the verbally dueling pair. "Would you like to buy the Whitman blend?"

Dax knew he impressed Taylor with his knowledge of the arts. "No blends of Adrienne Rich or Minni Bruce Pratt?" he fired off at the employee with a cocky smirk.

Despite herself, Taylor was stunned silent and slightly amazed at how informed and enlightened the pretty boy poet was. Not many people her age and not a filmmaker would know those names. "Right?" Taylor turned and smiled at the employee and held up the canister. "Yes, please."

The employee happily took the canister and headed to the front of the shop to ring up the purchase. Taylor started to follow behind. She hoped Griffin would like it, and even though she was worried about him, her day still turned out pretty good.

"Let me get you a gingerbread... person," Dax offered up, hurrying to follow her. He didn't want to miss an opportunity to spend more time with her. He wasn't making it a secret that he was interested in her.

Taylor paused and looked over her shoulder at him with a smirk of her own. "Fine," she capitulated and began to walk away. "But I'm paying." She didn't want to feel as if she owed him anything.

Dax smiled and followed after the beautiful girl. He'd take it. He watched the swing of her hips; he was definitely interested.

Chapter Fourteen

Griffin rushed out of the Uber car at the cottage and plowed his way to the embankment he'd gone down earlier that morning. He wasn't careful, and he felt a sense of urgency that kept him moving. He craned his neck and looked all around, searching the river's far bank fruitlessly. His heart thudded in his chest with a rhythm that screamed out, 'look-harder, look harder.'

He took off running again, toward the river this time. He hustled through the loose rock, bushes, and other obstacles on his way to where he'd thrown his hat out of the mounting emotions that he hadn't been able to control. He paid no attention to the slippery surfaces and crashed around crazily. He was on a mission, and nothing was going to stop him.

The closer he got to the water's edge, he began to slip a little and wound up on his butt on the cold ground. Pain shot like a spark through his tailbone and up into his spine as he landed with a thud. Griffin made a face, knowing he'd be bruised, but felt more determined than ever not to let his emotional mistake lose him his lucky beret. He'd need it for the finals. He resolutely pushed himself up and dashed toward the place he'd been standing this morning.

Inside The Hat Shop that carried more varieties than one would expect—with a large variety of novelty hats—one of the employees shook her head sadly at Roslyn and Alison. She apologized profusely, "The pancake convention was last week. We sold out all our berets. I'm so sorry."

Alison felt defeated and glanced over at Roslyn with a heartbreaking expression written across her face. She didn't know what else to do, and she knew how disappointed Griffin would be without his hat. Alison didn't think it was likely that if she ordered one online, it would get there before the next round of the competition. She silently cursed Jac for pushing Griffin to a breaking point.

At The Gingerbread Shop, Dax and Taylor sat at a table together, munching on gingerbread cookies and involved in a conversation about their lives. A typical first date scenario where each person did their best to get to know the other so they could tell if there would be a second date or not.

"It started when I was five," Taylor said to Dax in answer to his question. "I used to stare at movie posters. My mom, Ali, she asked what I wanted to go see. Anything I wanted, she took me. Million Dollar Baby. Eternal Sunshine of the Spotless Mind. Hellboy."

"You were five?" Dax asked, surprised by that thought. Hellboy was advantageous for a five-year-old.

"The Village. Phantom of the Opera. The Aviator," Taylor listed off with a smile. Alison fed into the passion Taylor had felt at that young age and helped her develop into what she was becoming. Yes, Taylor's hard work at being a filmmaker was because she put the time in, but she wouldn't be where she was with Alison backing her up all the way.

"Whoa." Dax looked impressed. There was a lot more to Taylor than met the eye. She was quick-witted, intelligent, and he intuitively knew she was creative.

"I loved the way images were used to tell stories. Sometimes with no dialogue, no narrative. Just visuals. That's how I knew I wanted to make film. If it's done right, it's universal," Taylor admitted with a sigh and a smile. It wasn't a chore to talk about her passion for filmmaking.

"For me, it was hard. See…" Dax trailed off and looked thoughtful, having turned inward for a moment. "I was good at everything," Dax said, making Taylor grimace as she bit into her cookie. That was where the confidence turned to arrogance. Dax grinned at her reaction. "And I had to pick *something*. So I picked poetry. Because it *really* bothered my dad."

Taylor laughed, and Dax smiled at the sound. "So you're not really a poet?" Taylor couldn't help but ask.

Dax shrugged. He was enjoying this time spent with Taylor getting to know each other. He'd told her some personal things, though mostly, he kept the conversation about him close to the surface rather than diving deep. "For now, I am. But when I'm thirty? I'm probably going to be an archeologist or a rock star or a brain surgeon."

Taylor laughed again and studied Dax's face. She

was utterly aware that she'd shared more than he had, yet she still enjoyed the conversation. There was just something she couldn't put her finger on that kept her from wanting to pursue things with him too much.

"I know what you're thinking," Dax teased, keeping the conversation light.

"What?" Taylor asked, schooling her face into a poker face. This answer should be interesting. She knew she was a challenging read for those who didn't know her well.

Dax lifted his hand in an 'it's simple' gesture. "He's got it all. Great body. Great Face. Great brain."

"But?" Taylor grinned, waiting for the punch line. Was he really that cocky and arrogant?

Dax put his hands down and leaned back in his chair while Taylor watched him. Confident and relaxed. "No but. I just know what you're thinking."

Taylor laughed, throwing her head back. "You're pretty ridiculous." Their banter was easy and relaxed, and Taylor found herself having a good time. She'd remain reserved, but there was no harm in talking with him about films and art. Plus, she was having fun.

"Ridiculously pretty, yes, I am," Dax replied with a charming grin. They both laughed, leaned into each other, and continued their conversation. They moved on to other arts than poetry and film, and the conversation flowed easily.

Griffin's shoes barely kissed the water as he walked along the very edge of the river. His face was creased into an expression of worry as he searched for the missing beret. He checked the ground, water, and shoreline everywhere he thought it could have floated off to with the current. The river wasn't deep, and he hoped it had gotten caught up in something and would stand out.

Through bushes and brambles down the embankment, he prowled anxiously, continually searching. The cold river rushed by on its journey to the sea, not caring that the hat Griffin searched for was carried off on its small rapids. The river had its mission: provide life and flow to the sea. Everything that didn't aid the river on that was inconsequential to the water.

The frigid slippery surface of the bank caused Griffin to stumble more than once, but he kept going. Twisted ankle, sore back, none of it would stop him. Ahead of him, he saw an overhanging branch that blocked his way down the river. He was sure if he could get through that, his beret would be somewhere on the other side. The thought stuck in his mind until it cemented itself as a sure thing. Griffin struggled with the tangle of branches and pushed through the obstacle impeding his path to success.

Without warning, Griffin's foot slipped on the mud and rocks, and he plunged into the icy water with a surprised and painful shout. For sure, he'd have more bruises now, was his initial thought. He did his best to scramble out of the water and had difficulty finding purchase on the wet and slippery rocks. The cold seeped into his bones and made movement more difficult as the shivers set in.

He wasn't foolish enough to think that hypothermia wouldn't be a concern, especially with the night falling around him, his distance from the cottage, and now, being totally and thoroughly soaked by the coldest water he'd ever been in that Griffin could remember. The cold had one benefit; he was numb and couldn't feel the aching pains he'd given himself throughout his searching for the beret.

No. Griffin needed to get up and out of the water and head back to the cottage where warm clothes, heat, and family would help him get through. Griffin clawed his way over the rocks. At times, Griffin stumbled on his hands and knees until he could push himself to his feet and get out of the water onto the bank. It didn't cross his mind that no one knew where Griffin was and that he could be in grave danger. He kept moving, slowly and painfully, but he was moving.

Roslyn paced outside Mozart's Steakhouse while they waited for their reservation, her cell phone to her ear. "No raspberry berets. Pink?" she said into the phone, voicing the color for Alison's benefit. The hostess called her name, and Alison followed her into the restaurant. She turned with a gesture for Roslyn to continue her conversation.

A few minutes later, Roslyn joined Alison inside, happy to be out of the cold. The sky was clear, and the air was downright frigid and left her chilled. They sat together on one side of the table that seated four, with five chairs around it. It was cozy, and Roslyn liked it more than she expected to. This little trip had delivered a lot of unexpected to her life.

"No," Alison answered Roslyn's questions about hat colors.

"Blue? Black?" Roslyn suggested as she seated herself and scooted the chair closer to the table.

"It has to be raspberry," Alison insisted. There were no other possibilities as Griffin was very particular and set in his ways about certain things.

"The kind you find at a second-hand store," Roslyn quoted the Prince song with a small smile. Alison playfully punched Roslyn in the shoulder. Roslyn was elated at the comfortable feelings between them.

"Ladies?" the server greeted them as he approached the table. "Can I bring you anything while you wait?" he asked, standing patiently with a friendly smile.

They hadn't even looked at the menus yet. Alison and Roslyn looked up, and then Roslyn glanced down at her phone, noting the time. "It's six now." Roslyn reached for a menu to take a look and see what the restaurant had to offer. "I don't know what Orion will want."

Alison reached out to push Roslyn's menu back down to the table. "Let me order for us," Alison suggested. She wanted to give Roslyn a break from making decisions.

Roslyn looked at her and realized that she hadn't let Alison pay for anything. And that Roslyn had been ordering her around most of the time. She wondered if this was what Griffin had been talking about earlier. Did Roslyn need to let Alison do something for her? It had been a long time since someone wanted to help her like that. She allowed Alison to push the menu down.

"That would be wonderful," Roslyn agreed, handing over the reins to Alison.

Alison smiled beatifically at Roslyn and then looked up at the server, patiently waiting for them to decide. "Can we have filet skewers and Parmesan garlic truffle fries for the kids and balsamic Portobello steaks for us? And sweet tea for everyone?" Alison asked as she closed the menu and set it back down on the table.

"Excellent," the server nodded and smiled, took the menus, and walked away to put their order in.

Roslyn nudged Alison with her elbow. "Did you just order me a giant fungus?" she joked. She was impressed that Alison had picked so quickly and decisively.

Alison grinned. "You're gonna love it," she promised. Picking food was easy for her, and she was thrilled that Roslyn had let her make the choices with no argument.

"Thank you." Roslyn acknowledged Alison with an intimate smile and contemplated her glass of water. She suddenly felt shy for no reason, and her stomach was a stampede of butterflies. "It's nice to let go a little. This has been... way more stressful than I thought it would be."

Alison listened attentively and patiently to the other woman bare her soul a little. It was beyond time, considering she'd probably witnessed Alison and Griffin at their worst in the short time they'd known each other. Roslyn needed to vent as much as Alison did.

"I've been divorced for two years. But last year, Orion got sick, and we couldn't come up out here. I hated that he was sick, but I was so relieved I didn't have to see Miles," Roslyn confessed in a rush of words. It felt good to air them.

Roslyn continued, seeing Alison's attention was focused solely on her, and she was listening. "Orion sees him every weekend, but Miles picks him up from school on Friday and takes him to school on Monday morning." It was an arrangement that had worked well for Roslyn, so she never really had to see him, and they only communicated when it was something that wasn't passed through official school channels.

"You hadn't seen Miles in two years?" Alison asked gently. It made a lot of sense, given the reactions Alison witnessed when Roslyn had seen the man.

Roslyn looked over at the other woman, unable to mask the vulnerability she knew was written all over her face. "Not since we left the courthouse no longer man and wife." Part of that was Roslyn's guilt over the marriage failing, and the way Miles had made it more complicated than it needed to be.

Alison leaned over and hugged Roslyn with a tight grip. One of those hugs that let you know you weren't alone and someone understood how you felt. The kind of hug that warmed your very soul. Roslyn's smile could have lit a dark cavern at the unexpected move. The stampeding butterflies grew in number when she realized she didn't want the hug to end.

"I'm so sorry. The last thing you need is me and my—" Alison began to apologize into Roslyn's ear. She felt so bad that Roslyn struggled with the emotions of seeing Miles for the first time after two years.

Roslyn cut her off, pulled back out of the hug, and put her hands on Alison's arms. She didn't want to, but Alison's warm breath tickling her ear had made her skin tingle and long for something that she knew couldn't happen. "Alison, no! Don't." She squeezed gently in reassurance. "Don't even think that. Meeting you," she paused to allow the words to form in her mind, "watching you with Orion. Meeting Griffin and Taylor. I feel so," Roslyn trailed off and lost the words she'd had a tenuous grasp on speaking. She lowered her hands from Alison's arms and turned away a little.

"Roslyn, what is it?" Alison's voice became concerned. It seemed odd that the typically blunt woman would suddenly turn reticent.

Roslyn was scaring herself. She couldn't look at Alison as she was sure that her face would give everything she thought and felt away. Roslyn had been about to confess her growing feelings. It was a sobering thought when she realized she was falling in love with Alison, and she believed Alison was straight. It wasn't often a straight woman would suddenly change what she was attracted to and then pick a practical stranger to begin a new relationship with, out of the blue.

"I'm sorry. I'm just—" Roslyn started to say, still not looking at Alison. She had no idea what to say to her.

"No," Alison interrupted defiantly. Roslyn looked at her then and saw a kind and sympathetic look. "Moms are supposed to help each other." She reminded Roslyn gently of the statement she'd made to Alison earlier.

Roslyn was silent for a moment. "I don't feel lonely with you." The admission felt like lead in her stomach, and the moment it left her lips, she felt naked.

"I hope not," Alison replied vehemently.

"I always felt lonely with Miles," Roslyn continued her open and honest streak. She could not stop, and the look on Alison's face did not say her thoughts were unwelcome, so why stop now?

"Mom!" Orion's excited voice interrupted their intimate moment. "Alison! I got a tattoo!"

Alison blinked, and both she and Roslyn turned to Orion in surprised shock, not sure what to say to that declaration. It wasn't every day you heard an almost eight-year-old say they got a tattoo. Alison walked over to Taylor, who was on Orion's heels and looked worried.

Call it a mother's intuition, but something wasn't right.

Roslyn knelt by Orion and looked at his face, which sported a Christmas-themed temporary tattoo on his right cheek. "That better wash off, Mister," Roslyn warned her son with a frown. She should've known. Miles wouldn't do something as outlandish as letting a child get a tattoo.

"Of course!" Orion smirked at his mom and rolled his eyes. She was such a worrywart sometimes.

Taylor and Alison walked over to the table where Roslyn was seating Orion at the table. "I've been texting Griffin for an hour," she told her mom worriedly as they approached.

Alison immediately pulled out her phone and dialed Griffin, shooting Taylor a nervous glance when he didn't answer. Griffin wasn't one to ignore phone calls from her or Taylor. Even Jac's calls he answered. "He's not answering," she said as Roslyn joined them. The anxiety in her voice was hard to miss.

Roslyn quickly caught on to what was happening after hearing that and seeing the looks mirrored on Taylor and Alison's faces. "When did you last see him?" she asked Taylor, jumping in to help.

Sitting where Alison had previously sat, Orion chimed in. "I saw him get an Uber at about one o'clock." Orion was happy he could answer, and he hoped that it helped make Alison less nervous, though he didn't know why Griffin taking an Uber anywhere would make them look like that.

The three females looked at the young boy and tried to piece together the puzzle they were missing important pieces to with shocked expressions. Something didn't add up.

Why would he do that? Alison wondered. Her mind began to spin fast with scenarios that scared the life out of her.

"I'll get the check," Roslyn announced, hurrying off to find the server. She didn't hesitate or appear to be bothered that their dinner was going to get cut short. So short they wouldn't even have food.

Alison motioned to Orion to follow her, and they began moving to the entrance to the restaurant. Orion wasn't sure why they were all so worried, but he did as Alison wanted him to do, took her offered hand, and followed. Griffin had been okay when Orion had last seen him. He'd just gotten great news and smiled at them and everything.

Chapter Fifteen

The not full yet moon hung heavy in the sky like a glowing lantern. There was the rainbow ring that was illuminated around it that signified the air up high was cold. Not like standing outside couldn't have told you the same thing, but it was a beautiful sight. The river could be heard flowing over the rocks in the distance, sort of like a babbling brook. It was a romantic and idyllic scene, if not for the worry expressed by the three women that flew out of the car once it was parked in the driveway, with Orion close behind them.

"Griffin!" Alison screamed, her tone manic.

"Griffin?" Roslyn repeated more calmly but still urgently. They searched all around them in the dark moonlight night.

"Grif?!" Taylor yelled, just as frantically as her mom. Her twin senses were tingling with a warning.

Orion was the only one who didn't call out. Instead, he stared out at the deck with a frown on his face. Something up there had caught his attention, and Orion paused to figure it out. His eyes narrowed as he strained to make out what the shape was that was on the deck. It was large but not moving.

"Mom?" Griffin's weak voice trembled out barely loud enough for Orion to hear. It was so faint he wasn't sure he had heard it until the shape moved.

"Griffin!" Orion exclaimed in alarm and bolted to the deck with the rest tearing after him. Orion's tone was distressed enough to spur all the women into action.

Griffin's cell phone was lying in a puddle of water on the deck, as dead as could be and possibly broken. Griffin wasn't too far away, huddled against the locked door of the cottage, soaking wet, shaking, and frozen. His teeth chattered, and parts of his hair were chunks of ice. The winter air was not forgiving.

The thunderous sound of everyone thudding up the deck stairs filled the otherwise quiet air and muffled the sound of chattering teeth. Orion reached the top first and threw himself at Griffin, knowing something was wrong and not quite sure what.

"Griffin! How'd you get all wet?" Orion asked, hugging him tightly. He was so cold that Orion grew cold even touching him. He was reluctant to let him go, suddenly scared for his new friend that felt like a brother.

Alison reached them next, sank, and gathered Griffin into her arms. "Oh my god," she groaned, panicking. He was almost catatonic with the cold, and she knew they needed to get him inside immediately.

Roslyn and Taylor approached and saw the situation. "I have an emergency kit in the car," she called out and raced back to the car.

"I'll get it," Taylor took off after her and motioned her back to get the cottage opened up.

Alison held Griffin tight and rocked with Orion

squeezing him from the other side. She was so relieved that he was alive after seeing the state he was in it was all she could do. Her body heat wasn't enough to warm him, and she wasn't about to let her son go until he was safely inside the warm interior of the cottage.

"Mom," Griffin mumbled weakly, his voice tinged with deep sadness. "I threw my beret in the river. I tried to find it, but I fell in." Griffin began to cry at the admission, the rest of his fragile sanity cracking under the strain of the past few days. "And I hate Jac."

The sound of Griffin sobbing made Alison clutch him even tighter. Griffin had never said he hated anyone before, and it destroyed what was left of Alison's heart. Taylor and Roslyn ran back up onto the deck, and Roslyn rushed to open the door and held her arm out to help Griffin get up and inside where it was warmer. Orion gripped Griffin's hand in his, his little teeth clicking with the shivers, as Alison helped lift Griffin to his feet, and he wobbled. There was no strength left in his body.

Griffin was so cold and weak from being wet in the frigid winter air. He could barely support himself. If anyone would let go, he'd fall again. The only warm thing on his body was the tears that spilled from his eyes. Luckily, everyone was there to help and ensure he was safe, and they showered him with love and care. He gave himself over to it; he'd never needed it more than he did at that moment.

Orion had finally fallen asleep after the rush to take care of Griffin, and Roslyn tucked him in protectively. It could have easily been Orion that had fallen in the river, and she didn't think he would have fared as well as Griffin did. Roslyn straightened and sighed, relieved that all the kids were inside and safe. She knew thinking those 'what if' thoughts weren't going to help anyone at all. They were all home, all safe, and Roslyn felt relieved it wasn't worse than it was.

She came down the stairs from the loft and crossed the living room. She hesitated only a moment before she walked to the master bedroom. She needed to look again to ensure that Griffin was safe, even though she logically knew that he was. She stepped up to the half-opened door and gently smiled at the scene she witnessed.

Griffin sat up on the bed, wrapped in layers and layers of warm blankets. He leaned against Alison, who had her arms wrapped around him lovingly. Roslyn didn't think she had let go of him once. It was a touching scene, and Roslyn was glad that it was able to happen after Griffin's harrowing experience. He'd told them he'd fallen more than once, and she knew he had to be feeling that as well as battling the cold that took root in his bones. It took a while to feel warm after something like that.

"It hurts so much," Griffin cried into Alison's shoulder, still shaking. He wasn't sure how he would get over this.

"Do you want more blankets?" Alison asked, misunderstanding what Griffin meant. She wanted to ease his misery in any way that she could.

"Not the cold." Griffin snuggled into his mother and clarified. Her embrace gave him more comfort than coming in out of the cold. The love she offered freely was what his heart needed to understand that he was still safe, even if things were hurting him.

Alison breathed in slowly, understanding now. He'd had a rough couple of days, and she was sure it all blended into his mind as an impassable mountain. "People fall in and out of love, Griffin. And it does hurt. And it's sad. No one falls in love thinking it will end." Griffin listened intently, and it made Alison aware of her tone. "But that's not how loving you works. We'll get through this. And I'll never stop loving you. Neither will Jac."

Griffin sat silently, and a few moments passed before he spoke. It was the things that Alison didn't say that resonated deep within him. He'd had a lot of time to think sitting out there in the cold. It was how Griffin passed the time instead of thinking he was going to die. He thought about things. "You don't have to defend her." He shifted slightly. "You can do mad."

Alison was taken aback by her son's statement and contemplated it. She had always been the level-headed one in her relationships, and Griffin was right. It wouldn't hurt her to be mad every once in a while. It might even help him to see that she felt anger and that it was okay to feel that way at times. Maybe if he'd seen her mad, he would know how to handle it better. It was a painful learning moment for her hand-delivered by her precious son that she could have easily lost tonight.

Roslyn was absurdly proud of Griffin, but her heart hurt for him too, and Alison. She backed slowly out of the doorway and left them to their moment. They had a lot of things to talk about, and it was between them. Her need to see them both safe was assuaged, and she needed some downtime herself. This trip was eventful in many unexpected ways.

Taylor stood down at the river. Her Super 8 camera was slung over her shoulder, more for comfort than any other reason. Sometimes, looking through a lens offered her a different perspective, and though she wasn't using her camera, Taylor believed a different view was what she needed. She felt on the verge of an emotional breakdown. The idea that Taylor could have lost Griffin weighed heavily on her. She sniffed, wiped at her eyes, and looked up and down the river. After a long moment, she reached into her pocket and took out her cell phone.

She scrolled through her contacts until the screen read Jac Wylie. Taylor exhaled a cloud of misty air, hit the call button, and brought the phone to her ear. After a moment of listening to the phone ring, she said, "Mom? You have to make this right." It was time for Taylor to assert herself on behalf of the others. Both of her parents had raised her to be a strong female, and she was going to prove them successful.

On the deck, Roslyn stood in a similar posture to Taylor. Her phone to her ear, listening to it ring. "Hey, Erik," she greeted her friend once he answered. "Do you still have your Prince cosplay?" It was a long shot, though utterly worth it if it worked out.

Taylor made her way back to the cottage, appearing out of the trees, and Roslyn saw the motion as she talked on the phone. Taylor's posture was a tad on the tense side, and Roslyn frowned. She worried how much the young woman could shoulder before she too broke down.

"And what about your Phantasma?" Roslyn asked, tuning back into the conversation. "That's awesome."

Taylor walked up the stairs and noticed Roslyn at the railing on her phone. She received a smile as she climbed, an acknowledgment that her presence was detected and not unwelcome.

"You're a lifesaver, Erik. Seriously." Roslyn ended the call and turned as Taylor walked up to her, joining her at the railing. Roslyn made a motion with one hand to indicate including Taylor in the conversation. "I may need your help tomorrow morning."

"Is it for Griffin?" Taylor wondered hopefully. She'd do anything to help her brother smile again. They could all use a reason to smile after finding Griffin the way they had tonight.

"Yeah," Roslyn nodded. She had a mischievous grin on her face that drew Taylor in.

"Anything," Taylor immediately agreed. She held her fist out to Roslyn for a fist bump. Taylor didn't even care what it was. Roslyn smiled and bumped fists, then clued Taylor into what she had figured out. Taylor felt a glimmer of hope and made her way to bed, looking forward to the morning.

Chapter Sixteen

Day 5

Over a wintry landscape with snow-capped trees, a drone buzzed overhead, startling the wildlife perched in the trees it passed over. The mad sound of flapping wings filled the quiet morning, drowning out the buzzing sound temporarily. The drone didn't falter or indicate that its path was interrupted and continued on its way carrying precious cargo.

Taylor was sound asleep, unaware of the drone's trajectory in her dream world until she felt her shoulder shaking. Like a switch had gotten flipped, Taylor woke up instantly and nodded. She pushed back the covers, and Roslyn saw she was already dressed. There was no wasting time with this young lady.

With a grin, Roslyn and Taylor silently descended the stairs from the loft. They headed out onto the deck without a sound the entire way. They waited patiently and stared off into the distance keeping a look out for their delivery.

Over the icy river, the drone flew toward the waiting women, who looked expectantly to the sky as the buzzing sound of the drone grew louder, a good indication that it was near. After a moment, it popped into view over the tree tops carrying a small package. It lowered a bit and hovered, then released the box. It was a fancy and well-loved piece of technology, and it delighted Taylor to witness it in person.

Roslyn quietly talked on her cell phone, confirming they had the package in hand. Taylor held the package and opened the lid, then smiled down into the small box. Her heart felt lighter and happier with the sight.

"It released the package and took off," Roslyn confirmed. "Should be on its way home. Thank you again, Erik. I'll make sure you get that extension." Roslyn listened for a moment and then smiled, happy that things had finally worked out.

Roslyn hung up the phone, and Taylor looked adequately impressed. "Erik Carlyle? The tech writer?" Taylor asked incredulously, putting the pieces together. "You know everyone."

Roslyn smiled kindly at the teen. How easily they were impressed. "There are perks to being a senior editor." Roslyn put her arm around the young woman, and they headed inside. The warm atmosphere enveloped them, and they began their preparations to cheer up Griffin. His laughter and smile had significantly been missed the past couple of days.

Roslyn padded up to the open doorway of the master bedroom. She didn't enter but instead watched the scene with a serene smile on her face. Mother and son were so peaceful and deeply asleep, she felt a moment of regret that they were about to interrupt that.

Griffin was still bundled up in the blankets with Alison's arms around him. They leaned in toward each other, and both were sound asleep. It didn't look comfortable for either of them, but neither had moved from that position the entire night, so it couldn't have been all that bad. Taylor sat down on the bed behind Griffin, causing him to shift, and his eyes cracked open. His waking movements woke Alison, who immediately turned her head to check on Griffin.

Taylor presented the raspberry beret to her brother and smiled widely at his surprised gasp. The sleep instantly cleared from his eyes. Griffin crushed the beret to his chest with a teary smile. Taylor's heart beat erratically at the joyous emotions that flooded her brother's face.

"You came home!" Griffin crowed weepily. He couldn't believe it. Maybe there was hope for the competition after all.

"How?" Alison asked with a voice still heavy with sleep. She was coherent enough to understand what happened, and her heart warmed seeing the joy on Griffin's face.

"It was Roslyn," Taylor admitted sheepishly. "She fought a heron for it."

Alison looked over to the doorway and saw the woman standing there with unshed tears in her eyes. Roslyn gave her a humble and happy smile. She guessed she wasn't the only one who missed Griffin's good nature and smiling face.

"Herons are horrible poets. They think good

things come to those who wade," she quipped, hoping to lighten the mood. There'd been enough heavy emotions to last them all a while. Now it was time for some laughter to bring life back to the cottage.

Alison stared in amazement at the resourceful and generous woman while Taylor and Griffin laughed lightly at the humor. *Thank you,* Alison mouthed silently to Roslyn. She had altered Griffin's life in more ways than she could know. Griffin had told her about the talks he'd had with Roslyn, and Alison couldn't be more grateful that the eBnB double booked their cottage this year.

"It's a Christmas miracle!" Griffin cried exuberantly. His emotions bubbled over again, only now they were on the sunny side of things and more in character with who Griffin was as a person.

Taylor smiled at her brother, beyond happy to see him come alive again. Alison hugged Griffin, and he, in turn, put the beret on his head, his smile enough to light the darkest of places.

Chapter Seventeen

Taylor, Griffin, and Orion sat along one side of the kitchen table, relishing a delicious breakfast of bacon, eggs, toast, and jam. Alison stood at the stove with Roslyn to her right. A cup of coffee in her hand and attempting to assist Alison. It gave Alison a first-hand view of how Roslyn worked in a kitchen, and though she tried to help, she needed help.

Eggs, a loaf of bread, and a jar of homemade jam sat on the counter like they were on a production line. "Who wants more eggs?" Alison asked and glanced over her shoulder.

All three kids simultaneously answered, "Me!"

Roslyn smiled at the kids, then over at Alison. "Three kids? You might be cooking all day." Roslyn stared at the food on the counter and sighed; at least she could make toast.

"I don't mind," Alison smiled happily. She honestly didn't. It made Alison incredibly happy to provide sustenance for the group and feed, literally, a basic need of life.

After a successful breakfast, Roslyn had started a fire in the fireplace in the living room to heat the house and listened to it crackle for a minute. It was a sound she always loved and evoked feelings of coziness and family. Satisfied, she walked back to the kitchen, where Alison washed the morning dishes and moved to help and dry them.

In the living room, Orion sat across the table from Griffin and Taylor. Orion's tinker case was opened on the floor next to him. The three of them played with three of the classic Lego Bohrok from the first generation of Bionicles.

Orion triggered his ball-shaped Bohrok and made it unfold into its robot shape like the others. They made the voices of what they thought the Bohrok sounded like and talked to the others. The teens were having a blast playing with what felt like a younger sibling.

Griffin heard Alison's phone ring from the kitchen, and he glanced at his as he pulled it from his pocket before sliding it back in, confirming it wasn't his phone. He was shocked his phone still worked after the beating it took between his falls and its frigid bath in the river.

"Hello?" he heard Alison answer. A few moments later, she came bolting into the living room with wide eyes and held her phone out to Griffin with excitement, her mouth formed in a silent 'oh' of surprise.

"Hello?" Griffin greeted. He suspected what the call was, but the notification of his progression hadn't been official. This call was the real deal, and the excitement would be no less than it was the first time. Only he wasn't alone and had someone to share it with other than the grinning Orion from the gazebo stage like before.

Alison and Roslyn both stood at the end of the couch and listened to Griffin's responses. They'd been waiting for this phone call. Neither woman had been aware that Griffin and Orion already knew that he'd made it to the finals. Of all the things to keep a secret, they held that news like it was locked in a vault.

"Yes, this is Griffin Wylie," Griffin responded calmly.

Taylor's eyes fastened to her brother with anticipation. The moment he broke out into a huge smile, Taylor wanted to jump up and cheer. She knew what it was about; she could feel it deep in her bones.

"Thank you. Thank you so much," Griffin said exuberantly. He lowered the phone and looked at Taylor first, then at Alison and Roslyn. "I made it to the finals," Griffin announced with pride. He didn't yell it or shout. He simply delivered the news with a mile-wide smile and a sense of accomplishment.

Taylor flew into action and crushed her brother in a hug while Alison and Roslyn cheered. Alison moved to join Taylor in their hug, and Roslyn sat on the end of the couch, not wanting to hone in on their family. The happiness and joy in the room flowed freely. It carried a sense of relief that lightened all their hearts from the heavy loads they'd been lugging around.

Griffin looked over at Orion and winked. Orion returned a smile, happy to have had a secret that only he and Griffin knew. It was like Griffin was his big brother and he liked that feeling a lot. It made him feel special and included in their family.

Dressed for the outdoors, Orion and Taylor stood on the deck, bouncing as they waited somewhat patiently. It was a perfect winter day, and their spirits were high from the morning's good news. They both expectantly turned when they heard the sound of the cottage door opening.

Griffin came out bundled in a half-dozen layers, including multiple coats, a scarf, mittens, earmuffs, and a hat with the beret balanced on top. He could barely move with all the clothes on, though he wasn't cold, which was a positive. He looked unamused, but the experience the previous day with the river had made him a little more susceptible to the cold, and Alison insisted.

Taylor and Orion tried not to laugh and instead exchanged funny looks with each other, and then they moved forward to join him. They sandwiched Griffin between them, and as a group, they headed down the stairs toward the backyard. It was time for them to do kid stuff now. Make snowmen, snow angels, have snowball fights, that sort of thing. Fun things that they didn't get to do on the other side of the mountains very often.

Alison and Roslyn stepped out next and turned to each other with proud smiles on their faces, and high-fived each other. They'd done a marvelous job bundling up the less than amused teen. Laughing as they spied the kids walking away, they went back into the warm house to enjoy some relaxed moments of silence while the kids played.

A horseshoe pole with two horseshoes lying on the ground near the poles sat empty, the shoes having missed their target. Another horseshoe soared into view and rang the metal perfectly. It echoed in the cold air and called out its victory.

Orion beamed a smile out, proud of himself. He pushed his glasses back up his nose for the sixteenth time. "It's all about consistency and the physics of the pitched horseshoe."

Taylor exchanged a glance with her brother and resisted an eye roll. "Science," Taylor whispered with a smile.

Orion proceeded to teach them how to throw a horseshoe properly, and they were all having fun, smiling and laughing like they'd been doing this together for years. From all appearances, they were a happy family enjoying their vacation. Orion wished it were true. He'd love to have a brother and a sister.

Inside, Roslyn and Alison sat on the couch. The fire continued to crackle in front of them in the hearth. Roslyn read a magazine she'd found inside the cottage and Alison was lost in a novel called Eternal Willow. It was toasty and almost romantic. It didn't take long before Roslyn was fed up with the magazine and tossed it on the table in frustration. Alison looked up in surprise.

Alison looked back to her book, then began to read aloud. Roslyn was touched and delighted that Alison would do such a thing to entertain her. Roslyn settled in, turned toward her, and listened attentively. More so, when Alison got to the steamy romantic scene, she needed a few more of those in her life. Hearing it read in Alison's voice only added good things to the experience.

A fire was roaring in the fire pit outside, heating the chilled air around the circular stone pit. The kids each held long sticks with gooey marshmallows on the ends and chatted amongst themselves. They were content to roast their marshmallows and sit under the winter moon. Alison and Roslyn sat on the other side of the fire and soaked up the camaraderie.

"It's barely eight, but it looks like midnight," Roslyn commented quietly and in a peaceful tone. It was nice out here without all the light pollution from the city and the sounds of nature instead of car exhaust and noise.

Alison nodded and smiled. She loved that about being out here. "No moon tonight. Too many clouds."

Griffin heard his mom's comment and looked over at her. "Mister Moon?" he tossed out hopefully.

Taylor smiled and nodded. Orion got a curious look on his face and wondered what Griffin was talking about with those words. The same look was mirrored on Roslyn's face. Taylor grinned because she knew what was about to happen.

Alison looked over at the other woman. "Do you like to sing?" she asked curiously.

Roslyn widened her eyes in mock horror and shook her head. "I can't sing. No range. A little pitchy," she half-joked.

"Do you *like* to sing?" Alison asked again with emphasis on the word like this time.

Griffin broke out in song, and Orion listened raptly to learn the words. He desperately wanted to sing it with them. It would be a first for him, singing around a campfire, only without the camping in tents part. It was too cold for that. Though, maybe someday.

"Mister Moon, Mister Moon, you're out too soon.

The sun is still in the sky.

So go back to your bed and cover up your head.

And wait 'til the day goes by."

When Griffin reached the last verse, Taylor joined in, and they were singing in a round. Their voices were clear and ringing out into the sky with the chant. It was mesmerizing, and Orion wanted to be a part of it.

"Mister Moon, Mister Moon, you're out too soon.

The sun is still in the sky.

So go back to your bed and cover up your head."

By then, Orion and Roslyn caught on, and Alison joined in, all five voices singing for the last line.

"And wait 'til the day goes by."

They all smiled at each other, then when they started back in, Alison smiled at Roslyn and joined in with Taylor, switching singing positions and the variation of the voices that sang together.

"Mister Moon, Mister Moon, you're out too soon.

The sun is still in the sky.

So go back to your bed and cover up your head.

And wait 'til the day goes by."

When Griffin reached the end of his second round, he sang counter-point, and Roslyn and Orion sang together that time. That was the fun of it. It changed tone each time, with people changing singing partners and harmonizing.

"Mister Moon. Mister Moon. Mister Moon. Mister Moon," Griffin crooned.

It was the perfect night, and they sang their hearts out until they were out of breath and too tired to continue. It felt like the night smiled with them when they finally headed back inside to sleep; like the stars knew these voices belonged together.

Three flashlights bobbed around in the loft with the laughter of kids accompanying them. With each light angled toward the middle of the ceiling, they were all together even though they occupied separate beds. The fun and optimistic attitudes hadn't left them, and now upstairs, they made shadow animals on the ceiling.

"Now I'm a bunny rabbit," Orion stage whispered and wiggled his fingers for the ears.

"Mister Alligator and Bunny are best friends," Griffin said softly, and they lowered their flashlights. He'd grown so fond of Orion that it did feel like they were best friends. He had a definite soft spot in his heart for the boy.

"Obviously," Taylor smirked good-naturedly with a laugh. She settled back into bed with a soft smile. "Goodnight, best friends."

Orion laid back with a smile. "I love having a big brother and sister."

Griffin paused as he made himself comfortable. He looked toward Taylor, surprised and touched by Orion's honesty. It was humbling for him to have an effect like that on a person. It made tears spring to his eyes. It was safe to say he loved Orion.

Taylor sat up and leaned back on her elbows. She looked between Griffin and Orion and spoke the words that got stuck in her brother's throat. "We love you, too, Orion."

Griffin nodded his agreement enthusiastically. "Absolutely."

oslyn sat on the couch with a gentle smile and an utterly full heart. She'd overheard the entire conversation, and she couldn't accurately describe how amazing it was to hear Orion speak that way. Roslyn looked over at Alison as she came into the room with her heart lodged in her throat. She was so beautiful.

"Did you—" Alison began, holding out a gift basket in front of her. It contained a bottle of wine, two plastic wine glasses, and a box of chocolates. "Hear a delivery truck?" she finished her question, wondering why the goofy expression was on Roslyn's face. Did she have some marshmallow stuck on her face?

As Alison sat next to her on the couch, Roslyn leaned forward and set the basket on the coffee table. Roslyn took the card from the basket and opened it, trying to calm down, so she didn't make a fool out of herself.

"I think it's from eBnB," Alison started sorting through the items.

"Yep. From Trina, our booking agent," Roslyn confirmed with a wry tone. "Hope the cottage turned out to be everything you needed. Don't forget to enjoy the hot tub."

Roslyn and Alison looked at each other blankly. Neither of them had known about the hot tub. But they each stood and headed to look for a change of clothes. It was an opportunity neither of them could pass up.

oslyn and Alison peeked out the back door. Roslyn held the bottle of wine, and Alison had the glasses.

"Hello," Alison called out in a low voice, greeting the hot tub with a sultry tone.

Alison set the plastic glasses on the edge of the hot tub that bubbled with warmth and now rainbow color lights that Roslyn had turned on. Roslyn poured the pink Moscato into both cups and then climbed into the tub wearing her white t-shirt. It was the best she could do for hot tub clothes; she didn't pack a swimsuit. She picked up her wine glass and sipped it as she stared out into the night.

"I do *not* remember this in the rental listing," Roslyn said on a groan as the heat soaked into her body. It felt sinfully decadent.

"It's gotta be new," Alison agreed and began stripping off her outer clothes.

"Wish I'd brought a swimsuit." Not that it had stopped her from getting in the hot tub at all. Roslyn looked over at the sound of a door getting closed. She wondered if Alison had gone back inside.

"It's okay," Alison replied softly.

Roslyn's eyes widened as Alison stepped into view and up to the hot tub, utterly nude. There was the woman of her dreams standing naked in all her majestic glory right before her. Roslyn opened her mouth to make some random comment, but no words would come. Her mouth went dry, and she had to take another sip of the wine.

Alison stepped up and to the edge of the hot tub. "We're both adults," Alison commented in a sultry voice like the one she had used to greet the hot tub.

Roslyn watched the curve of her calf as it slid into the water, her eyes slowly moving upward, memorizing every delectable inch as she sank into the water a lot closer than Roslyn would have thought. Wow.

Taylor and Griffin were sound asleep in their beds. Roslyn had checked before heading out to the hot tub. "I heard the kids talking," Roslyn managed to say after Alison was submerged. The interior lights still illuminated the beauty that Alison had in spades.

"The twins have always wanted a little brother or sister," Alison replied softly. She settled in so that their bodies touched.

The empty wine glasses—they'd already gone through the bottle–and the bottle sat off to the side as the women soaked. "You didn't want to have another?" Roslyn asked, genuinely curious. Alison was what every mom hoped to be one day.

"I can't," Alison answered sadly.

"I'm sorry." Roslyn curbed the urge to run a hand down her arm. It was so close. So tempting.

"Thank you." Alison gazed off into the night.

"For what?" Roslyn couldn't help asking. She wanted to know, and she also needed something to keep herself from groping the woman.

Alison looked at Roslyn with a grateful expression spread across her dewy face. "Most people say: At least you have two already."

Roslyn nodded in understanding. That would upset her too. "That doesn't make it easier."

"No, it doesn't." Alison was amazed that the other woman got it. Actually, she was amazed by her, period. She had been the entire time they'd been in that cottage.

The women sat in comfortable silence for a

moment. Roslyn looked away and then down and smiled to herself. "It's funny, isn't it?"

"Hm?" Alison wondered cozily.

Roslyn thought about the kids laughing and telling each other they loved each other. "Adults can be so awkward with one another. All wrapped up in pretense and assumptions. Kids make friends so naturally. But we lose that when we grow up."

Alison nodded her agreement. Roslyn looked up when she spoke. "We do."

Roslyn slowly inhaled and gathered her courage. She looked up at Alison. "Alison Wylie, with a 'y' in the middle, would you be my friend?"

Orion lifted a long string of copper wire and LED lights from his tinker case. He smiled a little and looked off into the quiet cabin. Orion was going to create some ambiance for his mom and Alison and hoped they would like it. He knew what romance was and knew his mom craved some of it. He'd heard her say so before his parents divorced.

Alison looked toward Roslyn. "Roslyn Wiley, with a 'y' at the end," Alison breathed out softly, "I like it when you say my name."

"Alison..." Roslyn stopped breathing for a moment as Alison gazed at her with open attraction. Was it even possible for her to feel that way?

Their faces slowly inched forward together, and their lips met with a passionate kiss. Roslyn lost all questions that had surfaced in her mind and lost herself in the feel of Alison's lips on hers. No way was she about to interrupt this magic.

A dark blue sheet dropped down over the railing from the loft and dangled. A small face peeked out from behind the sheet and between the rails to inspect his work. Orion had finished his little project, and he rather liked the way it looked.

The kiss Roslyn and Alison shared came to a breathless end, with their foreheads resting against the others. Roslyn smiled, dazed. "Does that mean you'll be my friend?" Her hopeful tone hung between them.

"Is that really what you want?" Alison pushed back, her tone suggestive.

Alison stood and reached for Roslyn's hand. She led her out of the hot tub, wrapped towels around them both, and into the house. Alison inched them to the space at the bottom of the stairs. They were holding their clothes in their arms, dripping wet. Despite that, they managed another heated kiss with enough fire to just about dry them.

Once they broke apart, Alison led them up the stairs to her bedroom and walked backward, pulling Roslyn with her. Suddenly, she stopped and gaped in confusion at what she saw.

Roslyn wondered what made Alison stop, and she slowly turned around to see a dark blue sheet draped over the loft railing with sparkling LED lights spread out across it. She guessed if the moment were going to be interrupted, that was a good enough reason.

Setting their clothes down, Roslyn and Alison came around the sheet and stared in wonderment. "It's like stars," Roslyn murmured softly. There wasn't a doubt in her mind that Orion was behind it either. He was an extraordinary child, and she was beyond blessed.

Feeling the romance, Alison walked into Roslyn's arms and gazed deeply into her eyes. "The heavens never felt closer."

Roslyn lost herself in Alison's eyes; there was no denying it now. She'd fallen hopelessly in love with Alison. The woman wasn't even legally divorced yet, and Roslyn didn't want to rush her, especially considering that Alison might never have been with a woman before. One bad experience might ruin her chances with her forever.

They stood under the cascade of lights, and Roslyn reached out to touch Alison's face. She trailed her fingers slowly down her cheek and couldn't help but feel happier than she'd felt in longer than two years. Roslyn became so lost to the moment she never noticed Orion's smiling face that peered down at them.

"Don't sleep on the couch," Alison whispered passionately.

"I don't want to rush you," Roslyn protested weakly. She knew there was zero chance that she would say no to this woman's offer. Not now. She was thoroughly caught up in the moment.

Alison pulled Roslyn into the bedroom. "There's room," Alison insisted, with heat to her voice.

"Just sleep," Roslyn agreed thinly. Her frayed thread of control unraveled further.

"Just sleep," Alison responded with a smile that indicated anything but sleep. She pushed Roslyn further into the room and made sure the door shut. "Roslyn?"

"Yes?" Roslyn asked breathlessly. She'd agree to anything at this point.

"Jac is short for Jacqueline," Alison admitted with another smile. She still wasn't sure how Roslyn hadn't figured it out, but she hoped that this solved any internal struggles she had going on as far as Alison was concerned.

"Oh." Roslyn didn't even mask her surprise. Alison laughed lightly, and Roslyn realized that the humor was in her response to Alison's confession. This time Roslyn smiled equally as wicked as Alison's. "Oh!" It was going to be a great night.

Chapter Eighteen

Day 6

At the top of the loft stairs, a robotic alarm blared out its wake-up call. After a moment, a small vehicle rolled toward the stairs with a whirring sound, and the alarm stopped. Then the sound of a robot tumbling down the stairs filled the air, and the whirring began again. A few seconds later, a small robot rolled down the hallway past the kitchen.

In the master bedroom, Roslyn and Alison slept facing each other, both wearing pajamas. After their fun that had been insisted upon, no one wanted any awkward encounters with kids walking in. The robot whirred its way into the bedroom, unbeknownst to the sleeping women.

Upstairs, the twins were woken by Orion's worried cry. "I think he fell down the stairs!"

"It's okay. He's a robot. He's tough," Taylor tried to reassure the worried boy as she got up and wiped the sleep from her eyes.

Griffin, Taylor, and Orion thudded down the stairs to check on the robot and saw the blue sheet of cascaded stars.

"Orion. Did you make that?" Taylor asked in wonder, the robot momentarily forgotten.

"It's really cool," Griffin said in awe.

"It's stars," Orion stated plainly, in case they didn't get it.

"I love it," Griffin declared.

The sound of the robot's alarm shattered the admiration and woke Roslyn and Alison out of their dead sleep. The three kids skidded into the bedroom, following the sound. Orion bent over and tapped the robot, silencing the alarm.

"It still works," Orion breathed out in relief. He hadn't worried about walking into anything uncomfortable. His concern was all for the robot.

Taylor and Griffin stood in the doorway with smiles plastered on their faces. Orion wasn't surprised since that's the reason he made the stars, but Taylor and Griffin were.

Taylor couldn't help the smirk on her face. "Apparently."

Roslyn and Alison exchanged sleepy glances and shy smiles as they sat up and faced their audience and the little noisy robot Orion created. Both women let out little nervous laughs, unsure of what to say or how to act.

That night, people gathered all around the length of the crowded park. A larger audience huddled in front of the gazebo. The easel with the sign that announced the Orion Poetry Festival Teen Poetry Competition Finals tonight was proudly displayed. The judges were seated with their clipboards and notebooks, ready and eager to listen to the finalists.

Dax leaned against a tree, as cool as always, and looked badass. A gaggle of teen poets slid past him with star-struck looks plastered on their faces. Dax grinned at them and tipped his chin in a greeting. His cockiness was at an all-time high.

Miles stood with his microphone near the gazebo, speaking to some of the contestants. Three teen poets, Sophia Eastwood, Lily Sustina, and Crista Camila Grace, stood close by and chatted him up. Miles smiled at them, amused at the behavior and the silly flirting. He wasn't unkind, just very aware that every young poet had a crush on him.

Roslyn, Orion, and Alison stood together near the front of the crowd. Orion had hand-drawn a sign that read Team Griffin with a little picture of Griffin, with hearts and stars.

Farther away near the edge of the crowd where things were quieter, Taylor stood with Griffin. He was pacing, nervous, and simultaneously ready to compete. He clutched his poetry portfolio tightly. Taylor caught him and stilled him, putting her hands on his shoulders.

Taylor felt like she was a coach that encouraged her all-star player before the big game. "You've got this. You've had your poem ready for months—the one about the snowflakes. Just read from your portfolio. Look up every three lines," she advised, speaking to the ritualistic part of Griffin that came out for these contests.

Griffin was more than a little worried. "This isn't my real beret."

Taylor was surprised that he knew that. After a moment's pause, she confessed. "It's not. It's better."

She kept her hands on his shoulders and explained. "That beret belonged to Erik Carlyle. Tech mogul and professional Prince impersonator. It was delivered by," Taylor paused for dramatic effect, "by drone."

Griffin's face had morphed from worry to amazement, to shock and delight by the time Taylor finished her explanation. He was impressed once again by the woman. "Roslyn?" Griffin guessed.

Taylor nodded and removed her hands from her brother's shoulders. She straightened out the parts she messed up so that he was all put together.

"Hey, girl," Dax greeted Taylor as he walked up to them.

Taylor and Griffin both turned and looked over at Dax. "Oh. Hey, Dax," Taylor gave him a friendly smile.

"Here to cheer me on?" Dax openly flirted.

Taylor glanced over at Griffin. "Actually..." she trailed off.

Dax looked at Griffin. "Hey, I read about you in Beat Poet. You're the kid with two moms."

A pained look crossed Griffin's face. Taylor just looked annoyed. "Yeah," Griffin mumbled, his mood began to darken.

"He's not a kid," Taylor snapped out. She motioned to the three of them. "We're the same age."

"Are you two...?" Dax didn't finish the question, beginning to catch on that Taylor knew Griffin.

"We're twins," Taylor announced proudly and with a bit of snark to her tone. If he'd shut up and listened, he would have known that by now.

Dax was surprised and cocked his eyebrow with a smirk. "Oh." Dax gave them each a roving once-over. "Threesome?" he asked rudely.

"I'm out," Taylor and Griffin answered in unison. They both turned and walked away, Taylor fuming. There was the red flag she'd been looking for all this time. Dax just brought it out and waved it in front of her face and her brother's. She couldn't believe his nerve.

Dax stood there and watched them walk away. He held his hands out in question. *What? Was it something I said?* he wondered.

Taylor and Griffin joined their family, and everyone was all smiles and jovial. Griffin gave Orion and his sign a thumbs up, and Orion gave one back. Their attention was diverted to the gazebo as Miles began to speak and announced the beginning of the festivities.

"Welcome, everyone," Miles greeted from the stage on the gazebo with the microphone in his hand. "To the Orion Poetry Festival Teen Poet Competition Finals." The audience applauded. Miles smiled and waited for the applause to die down. "This year, we heard from forty-five brave and unique young poets. And from those voices," Miles gave a pregnant pause, "our esteemed judges selected twelve finalists."

"Several of our finalists are nineteen," Miles announced dramatically.

Taylor and Griffin glanced at each other, and she squeezed his arm reassuringly. Griffin exhaled a nervous breath. It was his last chance.

"So this will be their last year to compete." Miles looked around at the audience with a broad smile. "Let's hear first, from Dax Linn."

The crowd applauded as Dax jogged up the gazebo stairs and took the microphone from Miles as he exited the stage to stand on the stairs. He took his time and slowly looked out over the audience. When his eyes landed on Taylor and Griffin, he winked.

Taylor and Griffin were both surprised by the wink, but then Griffin listened to the poem—obviously a plagiarized version of Whitman's famous poem—and he became shocked and appalled.

"I sing the body electric," Dax recited.

"The armies of those I have loved
engulf me and I engulf them.
Together we corrupt and discorrupt.
Charge each other full
with the charge of the soul."

Roslyn, Orion, Alison, and Taylor listened to Dax recite his poem. All of them—even Orion—knew this poem was rewritten from Whitman's. Roslyn put her hands over Orion's ears, and Orion pulled them down.

"So is the female form.
A divine nimbus of fierce undeniable attraction.
I am drawn by its breath as if I were no more
than helpless vapor."

Griffin felt like this entire performance was sacrilegious. He's entirely speechless.

"So is the male form," Dax continued.

"In action and power as flush as in scorn.
Alive with in appetite and defiance.
The wildest of wild passions."

Dax spoke with intensity and passion. Miles stood with his arms crossed, unamused. The poem was different—very different—from the original, but not enough to mask what he had done.

"The man's body is sacred.
The woman's body is sacred.

And no matter who it is, it is sacred.
And each of us—no matter color
or age or creed—
belong here in the universal procession.
I sing the body electric.
It is the only body I own," Dax finished.

Dax lowered the microphone and bowed his head. The audience was utterly silent. The judges exchanged glances with each other over the apparent plagiarism. Taylor was confused and looked over to her brother, whose face was aghast.

"Did he just—" Taylor began.

Griffin interrupted and finished her sentence. "Plagiarize Walt Whitman? Yes."

Miles headed up the steps into the gazebo and took the microphone that Dax handed off when he strutted off the stage. Miles looked baffled for a moment, caught with his mouth hanging open, then he recovered and addressed the audience.

"Let's hear from our next contestant," Miles announced. Miles called Mikey up and handed the microphone off less enthusiastically than he had with Dax. He was still reeling.

"So we walk," Mikey started.
Around the block.
Up the street.
Down a hill toward the park.
Walking without talking.
Nothing to pass the time.
Time has no meaning
when I'm walking
with Grandpa."

Paul DeSalvo was up next after Mikey stepped off

the stage, and his applause finished. The microphone changed hands again as Paul began to recite his poem.

"He was your son.
But he was my brother.
Mine.
I waited and waited for him to come home.
But the only brother who came through our door
Was the new one.
The baby.
And I wasn't fooled."

Karrie Liam took the stage next and performed her poem for the crowd.

"I don't want to talk about
the boys who aren't to blame
for staring at my chest, my legs
my yoga pants.
I want to talk about
the teachers who
write these codes
so intricate and detailed
outlining what I can't wear."

When Miles called him, Tyrean Zane stood with the microphone and shared his contribution to the competition.

"I am proud of you.
Do you need me to say it?
I am proud of you.
You stand
despite every storm.
But prouder still
I am of me.
The me you made.
The me I made."

Ana Morris walked up the steps next after Miles called her name, and she took the microphone. The contestants were moving fast through the competition, anxious to get to the end to see who would win.

"You being you
stops me
from being me.
And that's
the fundamental
problem."

The audience applauded as Ana Morris walked from the gazebo and handed the microphone off to Miles, and smiled brightly at the crowd.

Miles retook the stage. "Let's take a brief intermission before we hear from our last six contestants. We have cocoa and cookies for sale to benefit the Live Poet Society."

The audience dispersed; some headed to the concession table, others just wandered. Orion, Roslyn, Alison, Taylor, and Griffin stood together, huddled as a group, and tried to stay warm. Roslyn blew on her cupped hands to heat them a bit. Everyone looked chilly, not just her.

"Who wants cocoa?" Roslyn asked, making up her mind.

All three kids responded as one. "Me!"

Alison and Roslyn smiled at each other, and Alison put an arm around Orion and rubbed his arms. Orion stepped into Alison, accepting the warmth she offered. She wasn't surprised that he wanted cocoa or that any of them wanted it.

"Three cocoas coming up!" Roslyn declared.

She made her way to the table that some of the

other audience members mulled around. Some of them bought cocoa and cookies, and those with the cocoa kept their hands wrapped around the cup for extra warmth. Roslyn approached the small black table covered in paper cups of hot cocoa and plated cookies. Roslyn offered a ten-dollar bill to one of the two volunteers and was handed a four-cup beverage carrier.

Roslyn was putting cups of cocoa into the carrier when Miles spoke from behind her.

"Are you gonna avoid me for the rest of your life?"

Roslyn stepped forward to meet Miles at the end of the table, not wanting this conversation to be overheard by too many. "I'm not. No."

Miles grinned at his ex-wife. He was glad that she was honest. "Erik told me about the beret. Is there a conflict of interest?" His eyebrows raised with the end of the question.

"What?" Roslyn asked, taken aback. The question irritated her to no end. It was annoying that they still had mutual friends, and she didn't like Miles' little know-it-all grin. "Miles. I'm not dating Griffin's mom." Even if she were, it wouldn't be a conflict since they were no longer married, and she'd just met Griffin this week.

"Oh?" Miles questioned with a smirk.

Roslyn's irritation didn't end, and she noticed that his amusement hadn't either. "Not that it's any of your business."

"I didn't ask, Ros. You just told me," Miles pointed out smugly.

Roslyn looked away for a moment, startled at the realization. She pushed him away from the table after the brief moment of reflection where she wondered why she had told him. "Speaking of conflict of interest," Roslyn lowered her voice, so they weren't overheard. She was pissed at him and herself. Miles still wore that amused expression she wanted to wipe off his face. "You still close with Tom at Beat Poet?"

"Of course," Miles stated, baffled. "We're in the same writer's group."

"How about you tell him that introducing a teen poet by printing that he has lesbian parents is a dick move. Ironically," Roslyn paused a moment. "And I've only known her six days."

"Again, Ros. I didn't ask," Miles stated, though his expression was less amused now.

Roslyn had had enough. She turned away from Miles and grabbed the cocoas and cookies to bring back to the others. She walked up behind them, handed them their beverage, and schooled her face into a careful mask.

"We're in the final stretch, everyone," Miles spoke into the microphone from the stage. "Let's have a warm round of applause for the final contestants." The audience responded to the prompt from Miles and broke out in clapping their hands.

Miles called up Winnie Edwards, handed her the microphone with a smile, and stepped back to the stairs. Winnie stood and looked out at the crowd, her face serene.

> "What I wanted was to change
> the world and everything in it
> because the world let her die
> without doctors or medication
> or pity or mercy.
> I wanted the world to burn."

Miles called up Joyce Carolle next and handed her the microphone. He purposely kept things moving at a clip.

"Text Speak.
It's what my mother says
I use everyday and not
in a good way.
She says I am
single-handedly
destroying the
English language.
She says I am
with all my gen
slaughtering the art
of the written word."

Next up, Crista Camila Grace stood and held the microphone with both her hands. She took a deep breath in before she began.

"Wake up!" she yelled.
"There is more to this world
than you ever dared to dream."

Sophia Eastwood waltzed up the stairs to the stage when Miles called her name next. She almost had as much confidence as Dax.

"Once there was a bird.
Who set itself on fire
time and time again
whenever it was bored
whenever it was done
it just threw itself away
and shed all connections
to burn and be reborn
as someone clean and new.

That sounds to me
horribly
irresponsible."

Baye Lee Echo stood with the microphone held down. She had a piece of duct tape over her mouth, and she stared out at the audience. The moment stretched on, and the audience watched in stunned silence. The judges had blank stares on their faces, waiting for something.

Baye Lee Echo slowly reached up and peeled off the duct tape, and lifted the microphone to her face. "Are you happy yet?" she blatantly snapped out in a declaration.

The audience applauded the performance. Roslyn, Orion, Alison, and Taylor clapped, too, though they were somewhat confused. Griffin's head was bowed to his chest, one hand over his face as he shook his head.

"I can't follow that!" Griffin cried quietly. She'd made a powerful statement in his opinion.

"Best for last!" Taylor argued as the applause died down.

"And for our final contestant: Griffin Wylie," Miles called from the stage.

Griffin took a deep breath and walked toward the stage. Taylor exchanged a glance with her mom and Roslyn and turned her gaze to follow her visibly nervous twin.

Griffin stepped up onto the gazebo, and Miles handed him the microphone and smiled encouragingly. He said softly to Griffin, "You know, the best poets wear pancakes."

The statement confused Griffin a bit. "But you—"

Miles cut him off. Underneath it all, he was a good

person. "I'm good, Griffin. But I'm not the best."

The statement flattered Griffin and touched his heart. It gave him the encouragement he needed to get up on that stage and finish what he started. Miles squeezed his shoulder, and Griffin finished climbing the stairs. Not with a swagger like Dax, but with his head held high.

Time slowed for a moment, and Griffin kept his composure. He walked to the center stage at the railing and held his portfolio chest level as he looked out over the crowd. Griffin glanced at the judges, then over to Roslyn, Alison, Orion, and Taylor. Beyond them stood Dax, and then he noticed Jac stepping into view.

Griffin swallowed thickly and lowered the portfolio. He lifted the microphone and inhaled through his nose to calm himself. Then he began, his voice strong and carrying to the back edges of the crowd.

"There is a space between people.
Unavoidable, unrelenting.
It deepens and broadens as we age
as we learn more about the world
and what it means to be alive."

Taylor noticed that Griffin had the judge's complete attention. He had captivated them; her heart soared for her brother, and pride beamed from her smile.

"It's a great divide," Griffin recited perfectly.
"A chasm where things—
sharp, ugly and foul—
collect to scare us
when we feel most alone.
But don't close your eyes.
Don't blink or you'll miss
the moments, the heartbeats

the random events
the words and the actions
that illuminate, ignite.
Her laughter.
His love.
Discovery and hope.
Truth.
Forgiveness.
And joy."

Griffin paused for a beat. Taylor's face bore an uplifting expression; Orion's was equally so. Roslyn and Alison listened attentively, and even Jac, who showed up alone, listened to her son. Griffin felt his spirits lift as he finished the poem.

"These moments are the stars," Griffin said with passion.

"That bridge the cold void.
That drown out the darkness and fill
the space between us."

Griffin lowered the microphone, swallowed again, and didn't know how to interpret the silence that engulfed the audience. Suddenly, the crowd roared with applause. Griffin was stunned, frozen in place, with his mouth open. He certainly hadn't expected that.

After a moment, Taylor couldn't wait any longer, and she and Orion rushed the stage, crushing Griffin in a hug between them. Both were overcome with joy for how well Griffin had performed.

It was more emotion than Griffin could handle. He began to laugh and cry all at once. The audience continued to clap, and off to the side, Griffin could see Alison and Roslyn standing there, beaming expressions of love.

Inside the empty cottage, the cascading lights glowed with magical essence. They were a testament to the love that had bloomed among the recent strangers turned friends, now family. Was it chance, or perhaps the universe working its magic in a particular way?

The front door burst open, and Orion flounced into the cottage carrying a large trophy topped with a victory angel. The rest of the group trailed in after him, not one unhappy face among them.

"We won! We won!" Orion crowed and did a little dance.

Everyone laughed and smiled along with the exuberant child. Taylor put her arm around Griffin for the hundredth time, and Alison and Roslyn smiled at each other.

Alison reached out and brushed Roslyn's hair from her face, and Roslyn's smile became forced. Alison frowned as Roslyn looked away, and she wondered what was going on. That wasn't like her.

Meanwhile, Orion began to jump up and down on the couch while he held the trophy. This celebration was for Griffin! He was too excited to worry about what his mom was thinking at that moment.

Exhausted from all the excitement, Orion snored, deeply asleep in his bed. Taylor was conked out but not snoring, and Griffin was sleeping with a smile plastered on his face and the trophy beside his bed, along with the sign Orion made.

Roslyn had her pajamas on and made the couch up with a sheet. A pillow and blanket sat nearby, ready to be put to use. Alison walked in, dressed in her sleep clothes, and paused to watch Roslyn.

"Did I do something wrong?" Alison asked finally, unable to figure out what had changed.

Roslyn looked up at her, set the sheet aside, and sat down. Alison took the initiative and sat beside her. Roslyn gave herself a moment to find her words. She knew it wasn't going to be easy.

"It's been two years," Roslyn began. "A little more. And I'm still running away from him." Roslyn looked down at her hands in shame, realizing how much work she still needed to do on herself. "I feel, guilty. I feel, like a bad mom and worse wife, obviously."

Roslyn looked up at Alison again, her heart on her sleeve, and she tried hard to clamp down the overwhelming emotions that cascaded through her. She wanted to blurt out her love and the impossibility of it becoming something.

"I couldn't stay with him, but Miles will always be in my life because of Orion. I need to be more aware of that. I need... more time," Roslyn admitted hoarsely.

Alison wasn't sure what to say to that. She felt a bit shell-shocked as she took in everything Roslyn said. Alison looked down at her hands as Roslyn continued, her voice a little gentler than it had been seconds before.

"And you're, not even legally divorced yet. You need time, too," Roslyn said with a heartfelt sigh.

Alison looked up at that, hurt and angry. In her usual fashion, she kept it hidden, and it didn't reach her voice or her eyes. "Please don't tell me what I need. I've been told what I need for nineteen years."

Roslyn understood better than Alison thought she did. "And that should make you mad. Take the time to be mad, Alison."

Alison swallowed, her throat feeling dry. She heard Griffin's voice in her head, telling her it was okay to be mad. After a moment, she spoke. "So you're making this decision for us."

"I'm making it for me." Roslyn knew that was how it felt. But in her heart, she also knew that it wasn't the entire truth.

There was a tense yet tender and sad moment of silence the women shared. Then Alison got up and stoically walked away to her bedroom. Roslyn watched her go with her heart in her throat and then looked at the floor. Letting go hurt, and this time, it felt even worse than expected, and it was as if she could hear her heart shattering.

Chapter Nineteen

Day 7

Orion sat in the backseat of his mom's SUV with his tinker case beside him. Griffin stood at the opened car door, smiling down at Orion.

"Then on Wednesdays, I have tinker class, and on Thursdays, I have piano because piano helps the brain grow," Orion relayed his schedule.

"You're gonna be really busy," Griffin replied, impressed and amused.

"So will you! You're famous now!" Orion reminded Griffin.

Griffin lightly laughed as Taylor stepped up to the door. "Don't give him a big head, Orion. His pancake won't fit." Orion giggled, and Taylor walked over to their vehicle and loaded her bags. She didn't want to say goodbye.

Roslyn and Alison each exited the cottage, not speaking or even looking the other's way. They carried their bags, went to each of their vehicles, and loaded the luggage; it was a tense and thick feeling and didn't escape Taylor's notice.

Roslyn walked to the back of her SUV, and Alison went to hers. Taylor moved her bags around to help make room for the rest and idly listened to the conversation going between Griffin and Orion and all the classes that Orion would take. Taylor glanced at Alison, who positioned her luggage in the back, then glanced over at Roslyn.

Taylor sighed and walked over to Roslyn. "Roslyn?" When Roslyn glanced up and smiled at her, Taylor continued. "There's this thrift store by our house that sells tons of weird gadgets and gizmos and stuff. I wanna send Orion a little package. Would that be okay?"

"Of course!" Roslyn was a little shocked that Taylor felt she had to ask. "Hang on." Roslyn walked to the front of her SUV, grabbed a piece of paper and a pen from her purse. She scrawled down their address and brought it back to the patiently waiting young woman. "Here's our address."

Taylor took the offered paper and looked down at it. It was sitting on top of a copy of Storyteller. It hit Taylor then that Roslyn had gone back to the bookstore and bought the expensive book for her. She clutched it to her body in shock and reverence.

"I—" Taylor was at a loss for words.

"That's the book, right? The one you saw at the reading?" Roslyn asked, worried she'd gotten the wrong one.

"Yes!" Taylor cried, overwhelmed. "Roslyn, thank you!" Taylor stared at the book. "She's an indie filmmaker. Never went to film school. Didn't listen to anyone else. She made films her own way and they're...

they're so raw and real." Taylor looked up at Roslyn then, a shy expression across her face. "I wanna be her when I grow up."

Roslyn smiled gently. She remembered when she had that fire and passion when she was a teenager. Those were the days when dreams felt more attainable. "I think being you would be better."

Taylor stared at the other woman for a moment, then crushed Roslyn with a hug. Roslyn let out a light laugh and hugged Taylor back tightly.

"Shotgun!" Griffin yelled out.

Taylor looked back over her shoulder toward her brother. "No way!" She released Roslyn and dashed after Griffin.

Roslyn felt Alison's eyes and knew she was being watched. She didn't turn immediately. Instead, Roslyn kept the smile on her face as Taylor and Griffin play fought over who got shotgun. Then she looked at the woman who'd stolen her heart, and Roslyn's face became still and serious.

Alison stood and stared a hole through Roslyn while she hugged Taylor. Her emotions were all over the place, and somewhere in the mix, she felt the love she didn't think she would. When Roslyn finally turned and met her gaze, Alison felt anger for a brief moment that turned to despair and warred with a bunch of other stuff Alison didn't want to process. She turned and walked to the driver's side door instead.

"No one gets shotgun," Alison declared, her tone snappier than she intended.

"Aww!" Taylor and Griffin groaned in unison.

No words were spoken between the two, and the stubborn women got into their vehicles and pulled out of their parking spots. One after the another, the two SUVs drove up the driveway and turned in opposite directions on the road. The parting of ways, hearts torn open, and three kids that knew their mothers were hurting.

Roslyn swiped at her cheek that had visible tears and tracks making their way down to her chin. Sticking to her decision felt awful, and the look on Alison's face didn't help the churning in her belly. Doing what was right was often the most challenging thing.

Orion turned and watched Alison and the teens he thought of as siblings drive away. He tried not to be sad because he knew his mom was, and he didn't want her to feel worse. Orion faced forward again and cast a sly look at her. He was worried about his mom, and, now that they were driving away and it was goodbye, he felt as sad as she was, and he knew that because he saw the tears. Orion missed Taylor and Griffin already. He waited a moment, then reached into his tinker case and removed his cell phone.

Alison drove, and it was evident to anyone who looked at her that she was nursing some significant sadness, but when you looked beyond that, there was raw anger. *How dare Roslyn make this decision!* Alison thought to herself. She did realize that her anger may not be genuinely justified but was long overdue.

Griffin and Taylor sat quietly in the backseat. Griffin wrote in his portfolio, and Taylor stared out the window, wondering how to help her mom. It was apparent to her what happened and that neither woman really wanted the other to leave. Yet both were set in their ways and difficult to sway.

Both the teen's cell phones dinged with an incoming message at the same time. The sound drew their attention away from their musings. They reached for the phones in surprise and looked at their screens. It was a group text sent from Orion.

I'm sad this was our last day :(, the boy had sent.

Orion stared at his phone as it pinged with a reply text to the group message he'd sent. They'd responded!

I'm sad too, Orion:(, Taylor responded.

Don't be sad, guys. This is the first day of everything that comes after, Griffin texted back, remaining positive. He had none of the traces of the bad feelings he had during the competition.

Orion looked up from the texts and reflected on the messages and Griffin's sentiment. He smiled, thoughts forming in his mind. *Yeah! It's not just up to the grown-ups. It's up to the kids, too!*

Taylor and Griffin sat with their phones, and they exchanged knowing smiles with each other and nodded. Their twin communication worked overtime.

Chapter Twenty

Orion sat on the floor in his bedroom and worked on inventions out of his tinker case. His cell phone dinged with an incoming message. He picked it up, read the text, and laughed, texting back. He loved that the twins kept in touch with him throughout the day.

Griffin sat on his bed and wrote in his portfolio. His phone was beside him on the bed, and when it pinged, he picked it up, smiled, and texted back.

Taylor was at her desk with her Super 8 next to her and her laptop opened to an editing program. She smiled and texted Orion and Griffin a return message and then returned to editing. She needed to keep going to make her plan work.

Roslyn held several manuscripts in her arms as she walked to her office. Her phone was placed to her ear as she once again talked to Willy Patterson. He was as needy as ever.

"Willy, it just sucks. It's formula. Generic. Bland,"

Roslyn pulled no punches.

She noticed a gourmet cookware shop and stopped dead in her tracks. She lowered her phone from her face and ignored Willy; her only thoughts were of Alison. Thousands of images flooded her mind: cozy breakfasts, the kid's laughter, sharing coffee in the morning. It took her several seconds to come back to herself, and she resumed her call.

"I'll fix it. I always do," Roslyn promised and ended the call. She continued on her way. She needed to clear her head.

Alison stood in her cute little apron at the stove, watching her propped-up iPad and instructional video as she cooked. Her heart wasn't in it, but her mind needed the soothing motions that cooking invoked in her.

"Mom!" Griffin's voice broke through her straying thoughts.

Griffin and Taylor burst into the kitchen in a thunder of footfalls. Griffin beamed, and Taylor had her arm around his shoulders. Griffin held up a copy of Beat Poet Magazine with his picture featured on the cover. He looked fantastic.

Alison excitedly took the magazine from him. "Oh, Griffin!" Her heart filled with joy for her son. Alison thought the feeling was a nice change from the anger and sadness that had dwelled inside her over the past few days.

Griffin's phone chirped with an incoming text. He pulled his phone out and looked down. He saw a text from Roslyn, and he opened it.

Just saw Beat Poet. Congratulations, Griffin. Orion

and I are so proud of you.

Griffin smiled down at his phone and was tickled and pleased that Roslyn thought enough of him to send him the text. He missed being around those two and wished that whatever happened between his mom and Roslyn would just get resolved.

Taylor diverted his attention back to the magazine by pointing out a little curl on Griffin's photo on the cover.

Alison smiled happily for Griffin and took pleasure in the banter between the twins and their excited talk. She couldn't help but feel a little sad too. Alison knew who had sent Griffin the text. She went back to fixing dinner and fed the kids.

After they ate and cleaned up the mess, Alison curled up on her couch. Conflicted, she stared at her phone. Alison considered texting Roslyn, but Alison wasn't sure if her message would be one of anger, reconciliation, or a plea. Frustrated and depressed, she did nothing.

Roslyn sat in her home office at her desk. Her phone sat next to her like an accusing jury next to her laptop; she couldn't stop staring at it. Roslyn wasn't sure if she hoped it would ding with a text from Alison or if she should text the woman herself. In the end, she did nothing, and it ate at her heart.

Alison tossed her phone onto the couch and walked away. The anger won out, but not by much of a margin. *Fine. This is what Roslyn wanted,* Alison told herself.

Chapter Twenty-One

Roslyn closed her front door behind her after she picked up the package that had gotten delivered. She paused in the foyer and broke through the tape. The box had come through the mail from Taylor Wylie at a Capital Hill address; she'd addressed it to both Roslyn and Orion.

Roslyn opened the flap top of the package, and inside were gears, wires, and gizmos for Orion and a DVD in a paper sleeve. Roslyn lifted the DVD out and looked at the writing that was done with a silver Sharpie. *For Roslyn, My First Film.*

Without watching it, Roslyn put the DVD back in the box and took out her cell phone without hesitation. She loved those kids so much already, and she missed them terribly. Roslyn dialed a number and put the phone to her ear.

"Jennifer? It's Roslyn Wiley from Blue Forge Press," Roslyn began to walk down the hall with a purposeful stride. "I want to talk to you about an emerging filmmaker."

Taylor walked into the house from getting the mail. She sorted while she walked and smiled when she came across a fancy linen card in a deep red envelope. *What's this?* Taylor wondered. It was addressed to her. It wasn't often, or ever that she got fancy mail.

Alison stood at the stove, creating a pot of soup out of several vegetables and spices. Griffin was next to her with his portfolio and talked to her about the newest piece he wrote.

"What about the last stanza? I think it should end with 'twilight falls,'" Griffin mused.

"I like the color imagery," Alison agreed.

A loud squeal from Taylor interrupted their conversation. She burst into the kitchen and waved the invitation around that Roslyn sent.

Alison grabbed it from her hand to see what it was and read it out loud. It read: *You are invited to the red-carpet world premiere of Taylor Wylie's first film,* Counting Stars. *7 PM, Sunday, January 27, 2019. Emergence Theatre. Guest host: Jennifer DiMarco.*

Griffin rushed over to Taylor and swept her up in a hug, beyond excited for his sister. Taylor was still speechless and couldn't stop the grin that had spread over her face.

Alison's phone dinged, then dinged again. She took out her phone to see who messaged her and felt her heart skip a beat when she saw Roslyn's name. It was a war in her brain; half of it wanted to ignore the texts, the other half couldn't get them opened fast enough.

The only time I need is time with you. I'm sorry,

Alison, Roslyn had sent.

A third text chimed in, and Alison felt the tears form. *Let's make this decision together,* Roslyn's last text read. Alison's heart thundered in her ears, and the anger that had been building in her heart began to dissipate.

Chapter Twenty-Two

The Emergence Theatre marquee was lit in bright lights and read: Counting Stars, Taylor Wylie. A robust audience dwelled inside and mingled in and around the seats. Dressed formally in suits, Roslyn and Orion stood in the aisle and handed out programs to the guests that entered.

Orion nudged Roslyn when Jac and Kiki walked in. It took Roslyn a moment to figure out who the woman was, and then she had to swallow her surprise and keep a poker face quickly. This night was Taylor's night.

"Thank you," Jac murmured as she accepted the program.

Roslyn nodded politely and looked back at the entrance when Miles walked in. She smiled at her ex-husband and noticed she felt less resentment than before. It was progress. Miles took his seat, and then Orion fidgeted excitedly next to her.

Orion gasped and pointed as Griffin and Taylor walked in. Roslyn smiled, seeing Griffin wore a suit and a formal black beret instead of his raspberry one. Taylor wore a stunning premiere gown and heels and had her arm looped through her brother's.

Orion bolted and crashed into the twins as soon as they started down the aisle. The joyful group hug between the kids warmed Roslyn's heart so much that she didn't think she could get any happier than she was at that moment.

Orion led them all smiling and laughing down the aisle to their seats. Roslyn walked up to join them and heard Orion talking a mile a minute about everyone who was there and how he had already picked out their seats, how excited he was, and how much he missed them. Roslyn was confident her overflowing heart was about to burst. Then *her* voice sounded from behind.

"Roslyn?" Alison greeted her softly and timidly.

Roslyn's heart stopped. She turned and realized immediately she'd been wrong. Alison stepped closer, wearing a beautiful dress that hugged her curves and accentuated her natural beauty. Roslyn was happier now than she'd been moments before.

There was no question. Roslyn was very much in love, and she was speechless. Alison took the last few steps that remained between them and smiled so beatifically that Roslyn wasn't sure if she was having a stroke or not. Her heart had gone from stopped to hammering in her chest.

"You look—" Roslyn started when she found her voice. It was silenced almost immediately when Alison interrupted with a kiss.

"Amazing. I know," Alison grinned when she pulled away from Roslyn.

The women exchanged knowing smiles, and Roslyn offered her arm to Alison, and they walked down to join the kids in their seats. Roslyn sat on one side of Taylor, Orion and Griffin were on the other side of her. Alison sat next to Roslyn right as the lights dimmed.

"Welcome everyone," Jennifer greeted the audience from the stage. "To the celebration of a new storyteller."

Griffin and Orion beamed smiles at Jennifer and Taylor, who gaped in amazement at her idol as she stood on the stage. Roslyn and Alison looked proudly at Taylor in her moment of glory.

"Taylor Wylie is only nineteen, but already she understands the importance of human connection," Jennifer told the audience. "As filmmakers, we're told to dumb it down. Make it flashy. Make it fit in. But our greatest storytellers didn't fit in. They stood out. It's not about getting rich; it's about being enriched. About enriching everyone our stories touch."

Taylor's heart and soul filled with joy and pride for herself. It was a defining moment in her life, and she worked hard to make it happen. She glanced over at Roslyn and her mom with love. Taylor was thankful that these women were a part of her life.

"Taylor isn't afraid to break convention and find her own way. Because she knows that the road less traveled," Jennifer grinned, "is the road that brings us together."

Alison and Roslyn looked at each other and let their vulnerability show in every facet of their faces. There was no hiding any emotions or holding back. Love shone brightly in their eyes, and it was a sight to behold.

Taylor's short film, Counting Stars, a black and white exploration of family and discovery, played, showing each detail of what Taylor had captured, edited, and used to create her vision. It was a moment that would be etched into her mind for the rest of her life.

Epilogue

Somewhere between the ages of five and seven, a small girl sat on a rock near a creek. Her name was Dezirae, and she was reading a copy of Beat Poet Magazine, the one that featured Griffin on the front cover. After a moment, she looked up because she saw something at the edge of the trees.

She got up and wandered in the direction of the object that caught her attention. When she got closer, she saw a raspberry-colored beret that had gotten hung up on a submerged branch. She stretched her arm out and gingerly plucked it from the water.

With her magazine under her arm, Dezirae straightened up and studied the hat for a second. She wrung it out and shook it a little, and then ran to her parents with the hat clutched in her hands.

"Mama! Mama!" Dezirae called out excitedly.

Dezirae's two moms, CJ and Mary Jo, sat together near the creek. Mary Jo had her arm around CJ's shoulders, and they leaned into each other. When they heard Dezirae's cries, they straightened up and smiled at their daughter.

"What did you find?" Mary Jo asked curiously.

Dezirae presented the wet beret for her parents to inspect. She was rather proud of it and the fact that she found it and retrieved it. It looked exactly like the one that the guy on the cover of the magazine wore.

"That's pretty nasty, kiddo," CJ told her daughter gently.

Mary Jo plucked it from Dezirae's hands and nudged her wife. "Nah. We could wash it."

Dezirae smiled from ear to ear, her face lighting up with delight. "All the best poets wear pancakes."

Michelle Lee is a Pacific Northwest native with a mind open to possibilities. Growing up, people often saw her with her face buried in a book and not much has changed. She's living her life dream of writing books that set her imagination free and explore the possibilities and mysteries she sees in the land all around her. Find novel-length works by Michelle as well as pocket-size novellas at www.BlueForgePress.com

Jennifer DiMarco is a *Seattle Times* bestselling novelist and Bumbershoot award-winning poet who grew up in the Pacific Northwest. She has written and directed more than a dozen feature films and more than a hundred short films. Jennifer's wife, Brianne, and their children, Maxwell and Faith, played Alison, Griffin and Taylor, respectively, in *The Space Between Us* and Jennifer played herself. Find Jennifer's books and poetry at BlueForgePress.com and find many of her films at BlueFlix at BlueForgeFilms.com

www.ingramcontent.com/pod-product-compliance
Lightning Source LLC
Chambersburg PA
CBHW071525120726
47907CB00013B/1076